Timothy Holmes

Sir Benjamin Collins Brodie

Timothy Holmes

Sir Benjamin Collins Brodie

ISBN/EAN: 9783337141707

Printed in Europe, USA, Canada, Australia, Japan

Cover: Foto ©Raphael Reischuk / pixelio.de

More available books at **www.hansebooks.com**

MASTERS OF MEDICINE

"HOMINES AD DEOS NULLA IN RE
PROPIUS ACCEDUNT QUAM
SALUTEM HOMINIBUS DANDO."
CICERO.

Masters of Medicine

SIR BENJ. COLLINS BRODIE

B C Brodie.

SIR BENJAMIN COLLINS BRODIE

BY

TIMOTHY HOLMES, M.A.,
F.R.C.S.

LONDON
T. FISHER UNWIN
PATERNOSTER SQUARE
MDCCCXCVIII

To

SIR BENJAMIN VINCENT SELLON BRODIE,

Bart.

IN GRATEFUL RECOGNITION OF VALUABLE

ASSISTANCE AND ADVICE GIVEN TO THE

AUTHOR IN THE PREPARATION OF

THIS LIFE OF HIS ILLUSTRIOUS

GRANDFATHER

PREFACE

THE great surgeon whose life I have undertaken here to pourtray has been dead more than thirty-five years. He was then seventy-nine years of age ; so that few are now alive who knew him in his vigour. I am not one of these ; but I knew him in later life, for I Had occasion, at the commencement of my surgical career, to experience the unfailing kindness with which Brodie always received and helped young men whom he had any reason for thinking earnest in the pursuit of the profession of which he was then the acknowledged chief. Gratitude for these favours, as well as an ardent desire to do honour to one of the great men who have adorned the hospital to which I am bound by so many ties, must be my excuse for undertaking a task from which Mr. Charles Hawkins, his intimate friend, and the editor of his collected works, shrank. Mr. Hawkins did not decline this enterprise from want of ability, for no one else could have done it so well, but because the very intimacy of

his friendship and the warmth of his affection in-
capacitated him, in his own judgment, from forming
"a judicial estimate" of Brodie's character. We
may regret Mr. Hawkins's decision, while we cannot
but respect its motives. It has, however, left us
without any sufficient data for the judicial estimate of
which he speaks. Our materials for the life of Brodie,
beyond his own works, are his Autobiography and the
obituary notices published at the time by his friends
and admirers, amongst whom Sir H. Acland is conspicuous, together with such reminiscences as can be
supplied by those who knew him, or are preserved in
the records of his family. These means I have used
to the best of my ability, and though I am far from
the presumption of aspiring to sit in judgment on so
great a man, I hope to put my readers in possession
of some idea of him who, of all English surgeons now
passed away, seems to me to have brought the most
acute intellect and the most powerful mind to the
study of surgery, after John Hunter. And Brodie's
life is perhaps more interesting to the general reader
even than that of Hunter, in this respect, that Brodie
was versed in nearly every branch of human knowledge, in all the highest kinds of literature, and in all
forms of philanthropy and social effort. His great
predecessor's "soul dwelt apart" from the ordinary
ways of men. Hunter went little, if at all, into
society, took no part in public questions, had no
knowledge of literature, and little interest in any
science except physiology and natural history. Brodie,
on the contrary, was not only the greatest surgeon

PREFACE

of his time, and one of its most accomplished physiologists, but also, as is well said in the Preface to this Series, by its editor (whose loss we have now to deplore), he was " one of those who most largely helped to transform surgery from a handicraft to a science " ; and his success and reputation did much to elevate surgery to an equality with the other great professions, and to qualify its practitioners to consort on equal terms with the greatest celebrities in the world of science.

I have tried in the following pages to set forth these various claims of Brodie to the gratitude and appreciation of posterity, how imperfectly no one can feel more than I do. Yet I hope that this book may do something to keep alive the memory of one of the most noteworthy figures of a past generation.

For permission to use the striking portrait which Watts painted in the year 1860, we are indebted to the present holder of the title, who also himself photographed it for our Frontispiece. Sir Benjamin V. S. Brodie has likewise supplied the account of the Brodie family in my first chapter, as well as subsequent notices of Brodie's life in society and in the country.

CONTENTS

CONTENTS

CONTENTS

CHAPTER VII.

CHAPTER VIII.

CHAPTER IX.

LIST OF TOPICS IN APPENDIX.

CONTENTS

I

1783–1805

EARLY LIFE AND EDUCATION, AT HOME AND AT ST. GEORGE'S HOSPITAL

Origin and History of Brodie's family—Brodie's father—Home life and education—Choice of profession—Early medical studies—Death of his father—His early associates and hospital work—The old hospital system; Brodie's views on medical education.

"Every Scottish man has a pedigree. It is a national prerogative, as unalienable as his pride and his poverty."—SIR WALTER SCOTT.

IT is unnecessary to say from which of the three kingdoms the subject of the present memoir derived his descent. The clan of Brodie has held an important position in the Province of Moray since the time of Alexander III. of Scotland, and its history is intimately connected with that of Moray and the immediate neighbourhood. Shaw, in his history of that province, gives as the derivation of the name an old Irish word Broth, which signifies a ditch, and is of opinion that Brodie received its name from a ditch in the neighbourhood of the village of Dyke. He adds : " Be this as it will the antiquity of the name

17

appeareth from this that no history, record, or tradition (that I know of) doth so much as hint that any other family, or name, possessed the lands of Brodie before them, or that they came as strangers from another country."

In the Covenanting times the clan suffered severely, and under the "Great Marquis" in 1645, to borrow the words of the Laird of Brodie, "We fell before the wild Irishes six tyms without anie interruption, and to mingle the Churches and the Lands calamitie with my privat my hous and my mains and bigging was burnt to the ground, and my estat made desolat and noe place left me, no mens to subsist : Leathin's (his uncle's) lands wer burnt, his hous, and my deir friend, and Christian brethren wer besedged, and blocked up, and in fear of their lyfes by Huntlie."[1]   It was at this time, according to Shaw, that the documents and papers were destroyed or carried off from Brodie Castle, thus rendering the history of the family more meagre than it would otherwise have been.

Nor was this all ; a few years later heavy fines were inflicted on members of many of the chief clans, and the Brodies did not escape, several members of the family being fined for refusing to conform to the Test Act.

The member of the clan with whom we are concerned, Alexander Brodie, himself the son of Alexander in Glassaugh, was born at Glassaugh and baptized at Fordyce, in 1701. Glassaugh is a small hamlet in Banffshire, near the ancient castle of Findlater, which

[1] Diary of Alexander Brodie, of Brodie, Lord of Session in 1649.

stands on that rocky coast, and is about four miles east of Cullen. One of the witnesses at his baptism was Alexander Abercromby, of Glassaugh, who had married a daughter of Sir Robert Dunbar, of Grangehill, and granddaughter of Alexander Brodie, of Brodie, the Lord of Session.

It is not a little remarkable that this Alexander, born in a remote part of Scotland, should have been the grandfather of two such distinguished men as Sir Benjamin Collins Brodie, and Thomas Lord Denman, the advocate of the unfortunate Queen Caroline, and subsequently Chief Justice of the King's Bench.

Alexander had a brother James, and a sister Isabel, who afterwards married Alexander Duff, and who, with her younger brother, migrated to the North of Ireland.

Before the year 1740, Alexander Brodie left his native country and came to London, having, as there is reason to believe, been involved (in those days of Jacobitism), in some political trouble.

He married Margaret, a daughter of Dr. Samuel Shaw, a physician, a relation, it is believed, of Dr. Peter Shaw, whose daughter married the first Dr. Warren, and who was physician to George II.

Dr. Shaw had followed the fortunes of the Stuarts, and if "I am not mistaken, had accompanied King James II. abroad. The supposition that my grandfather had become involved in some political difficulties is rather confirmed by the circumstance of his having afterwards married the daughter of a staunch Jacobite, and by the Jacobite songs which my

Aunt Margaret was accustomed to repeat to us when I was a child." [1]

This lady had very strong Jacobite principles, so much so that on the occasion of the baptism of her niece, the daughter of her sister, Mrs. Denman, she composed some verses in which she commented strongly on the choice of such a " Brunswick name " as Sophia being bestowed upon the child. For many years, and up to the date of his death in 1772, Alexander Brodie lived in a house in Brewer Street, in the parish of St. James's, Westminster. His wife was a person of very considerable abilities, and her letters to her daughter show not only that she was well educated, but also that she and her husband moved in good society. He had two sons and five daughters; the youngest daughter, however, must have died young, since Dr. Denman mentions his wife, at the time of her marriage in 1770, as being the youngest. Samuel, the younger son, left England in 1769, for India, in a ship called the *Lord Holland;* the ship appears to have been lost at sea, and he himself was either lost with her or died in India.

Peter Bellinger Brodie, the elder son, was born in 1742. He obtained a nomination on the foundation of the Charterhouse in 1756, and from thence obtained an exhibition at Worcester College, Oxford. " As a boy he was patronised by the first Lord Holland, and passed much of his time at Holland House." The exact date when the acquaintance with the Fox

[1] This and other similar quotations are from the autobiography of Sir Benjamin Brodie.

family began is uncertain, but letters exist which show that it was previous to the year 1758. He was ordained immediately after leaving Oxford, and when the second lord purchased the estate and mansion at Winterslow, in Wiltshire, he rented a cottage in the same place, in order that he might be near him. He assisted Lord Holland, to whom, as well as to his brother, Charles James Fox, he was sincerely attached, in planting and generally improving the estate, and from letters which he wrote at that time to his sister, he appears to have been almost constantly with one or other of the brothers.

Shortly after Lord Holland's death in 1774, a vacancy occurred in the living of Winterslow, and in accordance with the directions contained in his will, it was offered to Mr. Brodie, and he became Rector of Winterslow, the only preferment he ever received. A near connection with Mr. Fox was not in those days a good passport to high places in the Church, so Mr. Brodie had to content himself with the care of this little parish of between 700 and 800 souls, his duties as a Magistrate and Deputy Lieutenant, and the education of his children. In the year 1775 he married Sarah, daughter of Benjamin Collins, of Milford, near Salisbury. This gentleman, who was a banker and printer, bought from Goldsmith in the year 1762 a third share of the "Vicar of Wakefield," for twenty guineas.[1] The sale took place on the 28th of October, but whether at London or Salisbury, is uncertain. On 26th of March, 1766, "The Vicar of

---

[1] " Life of Goldsmith," by Austin Dobson.

Wakefield" appeared, the imprint being "Salisbury : Printed by B. Collins, for F. Newbery, in Pater Noster Row." There is a portrait of Benjamin Collins in the possession of Mr. Alexander Brodie. Mr. Brodie himself, was a good scholar, a man of much sense, attached to his family, and competent to give his children good instruction ; and they had no other tutor. He gave them, moreover, what was better than mere instruction. He conveyed, at least to the subject of this memoir, that lifelong pleasure in study which is far above all technical education, that interest in all the arts and sciences by which Brodie was distinguished from the ordinary run of surgical practitioners, and that love of whatever is noble and of good repute which earned for him the universal respect of his contemporaries. The affection which the son felt for his father shines out throughout the early part of the Autobiography. His mother's character is not brought out so strongly, but he speaks of her in very high terms. She long survived her husband, dying at the age of ninety-two in 1847, and some letters written by her in that year show how very perfectly she retained her faculties, though she had reached so great an age.

The family at Winterslow consisted of two daughters and four sons of whom the subject of this memoir was the third. Mr. Brodie sent none of his sons to a public school or to either of the Universities, but he kept them well to their work, and they learned probably as much if not more of Latin, Greek, and Mathematics, than they would have done at Eton or Oxford : "But there were undoubtedly disadvantages belonging to this kind of life. We had much to learn," says Sir Benjamin, "when we came into the world, which others learn as boys at Eton, or Harrow, or Rugby. In my own case one [disadvantage] was a shyness in general society which for a long time was very oppressive, and which it took many years for me to overcome ; and another was that not having sufficient opportunities of comparing myself with others, I formed no right estimate of my own character, over-rating myself in some things, and underrating myself in others." But the whole of this account of his boy-hood at Winterslow shows that it was a round of strenuous industry, of simple pleasures and elevated pursuits—a very fit introduction to a life of honour-able ambition and the active prosecution of a noble calling.

The story of Brodie's early days presents him in a character which those who knew him only in his old age would never have anticipated, viz., as a soldier. In that period of excitement and alarm when a French invasion was not only thought probable, but was actually contemplated by the greatest captain of his time, nearly every one took up arms, and amongst these were the three brothers, Peter, William, and Benjamin Brodie; who in 1798 raised a company of Volunteers, which at last attained the number of 140. The second of the three—the captain—was only 18 years old, and Brodie himself who was ensign, only 14. They seem to have worked heartily at their duty ; and they succeeded in obtaining for their corps the credit of being the best drilled and best disciplined in that part of the country.[1] We can easily believe that the same spirit of thoroughness which he showed in after life animated Brodie and his brothers in this youthful adventure.

Nor does he seem to have pursued his literary studies negligently. I found among Sir Benjamin's papers an old copybook in a handwriting which though it shows traces of his well-known MS. is in a very different character from that in which, evidently at a late period of his life, he has noted the date of its composition. That date is July, 1802—in his 19th year. It is a translation of the 'Ερασταί, one of Plato's minor dialogues. I took the trouble of comparing the translation line for line with the original. It is not faultless. One or two absolute errors can be detected, and it gives here and there rather the author's general meaning than a rendering of his words; but it shows a knowledge of Greek which few lads of 18 possess who are not studying for any examination, and a love of literature which is, I think, still rarer at that age. The subject of the dialogue had, I daresay, an attraction for one of Brodie's practical sense and interest in affairs, since its scope is to show that philosophy is less concerned with acquiring a knowledge of the arts and sciences than in fitting a man for managing the

[1] The commission is yet in existence, signed by King George III., appointing "Our trusty and well beloved Benjamin Collins Brodie, gent., Ensign in the company of the Winterslow, Pitton, Farley, East Grimstead, and Dean Volunteers, commanded by our trusty and well beloved captain, William Brodie." It is dated October 3, 1799.

business of life and serving his friends or the State—a practical philosophy in which few men have ever surpassed him.

The way in which they were kept to their work would perhaps astonish many children of the present day. "As long as I can remember anything, my father always endeavoured to impress on our minds that we should have to obtain our livelihood by our own exertions ; that he would do his utmost to give us a good education, to accustom us to industrious habits, and put us in the way of providing for ourselves ; but that he could do nothing more. In the summer my brothers and myself rose at six o'clock, and two hours were devoted to study, generally learning to repeat Greek and Latin poetry, or Cicero's Orations before we breakfasted at half-past eight o'clock. Immediately after breakfast we resumed our studies ; we dined at three o'clock, and were then at our studies again from four to six o'clock. In the winter our hours of study were somewhat different ; and from eight to half-past nine o'clock, my father read some book of amusement or instruction aloud to the whole family. On two days in the week when my father was absent on public business, we had half-holidays. We had no other vacations during the whole year except on some grand occasion, such as a cricket match or the first few days of the skating season."

But if their hours of study were long, they had recreation as well, as the following play-bill testifies :—

BRODIE

At Winterslow.

On Wednesday, August 26th, 1789, will be presented
The Tragedy of
Phædra and Hippolitus.

Theseus	Mr. Brodie, jun.
Hippolitus	Mr. Denman.
and	
Lyton	Mr. Brodie, sen.

To which will be added
Three Weeks after Marriage.

Sir Charles Racket	Mr. Denman
Footman	Mr. B. Brodie
Drugget	Mr. Brodie, sen.
Woodley	Mr. Brodie, jun.
Lady Racket	Mr. Holloway, jun.

N.B.—The doors will be opened at a quarter after
five, and the Performance to begin at a quarter
before six.

In after years this playbill was shown to Mr. W. B.
Brodie, the "Mr. Brodie, jun.," of the Dramatis
Personæ, and with reference to it he said, "I remember the little event as vividly as if it had occurred only
yesterday, particularly the very spirited way in which
Mr. Denman acted Sir Charles Racket. He was a
remarkably intelligent boy." In the year of this little
performance, the future Chief Justice of the King's
Bench was not yet eleven years old, having been born
in 1779.

Considering the many connections which the
Brodie family had with leading medical men, it would
have been strange if none of the sons had embraced
the profession of medicine. The eldest, Peter, was
bred up to the law, and obtained a very high standing

as a conveyancer, the Act (3 and 4 Will. IV., c. 74), which bears his name, for the abolition of Fines and Recoveries being a real masterpiece of drafting. The second, William, was led, by the success of some members of his mother's family in commerce at Salisbury, to join them in business there, and became a successful banker and member of Parliament, though he afterwards met with reverses. The youngest son joined his brother William, and became Mayor of Salisbury. He was also a member of the Volunteer corps mentioned on page 23. He was the father of the distinguished accoucheur, Dr. G. Brodie. So, as his elder brothers were otherwise provided for, Benjamin was sent to London to study medicine. His connexions there were indeed good. Dr. Denman had married his aunt. Dr. Baillie (Hunter's nephew) and Sir Richard Croft (the leading accoucheur of the day) had each married one of his cousins. He had friends, therefore, in the highest ranks of medical society ; and he had also excellent introductions into the legal and other circles through his brother and his cousin, the future Lord Denman.

Brodie tells us plainly that he had no especial taste or desire for the profession in which he became so eminent. "Others," he writes, "have often said to me that they supposed I must have had, from the first, a particular taste or liking for my profession ; but it was no such thing : nor does my experience lead me to have any faith in those special callings to certain ways of life which some young men are supposed to have. . . . The persons who succeed best in professions are those who, having (perhaps from some accidental circumstance) been led to embark in them, persevere in their course as a matter of duty, or because they have nothing better to do. They often feel their new pursuit to be unattractive enough in the beginning, but as they go on, and acquire knowledge, and find that they attain some degree of credit, the case is altered, and from that time they become every day more interested in what they are about. There is no profession to which these observations are more applicable than they are to the medical. The early studies are, in some respects, disagreeable to all, and to many repulsive. But, in the practical exercise of its duties in the hospital, there is much that is of the highest interest ; and the collateral sciences, to those whose position gives them the opportunity of cultivating them, offer at least as much to gratify our curiosity and excite our admiration as any other branches of knowledge, not even excepting the sublime investigations of astronomy."[1]

Brodie is of course speaking of the ordinary profession, not of callings such as painting or music, which require tastes and even faculties not given to everybody ; and with that obvious limitation his opinion is eminently just and wise. He himself would, no doubt, have followed his father's profession with content and success, and possibly with as high distinction as he attained in surgery.

For some time after he commenced his medical studies, he would willingly have embraced a different

[1] See Appendix A, Brodie on Choice of a Profession.

career. "I worked hard enough," he says, "but it was rather as a matter of duty, or rather, I ought to say, of necessity, than because I felt any very great interest in what I was doing; and most willingly, if I could have afforded it, would I have turned my back on anatomy and returned to literary pursuits." It was not merely the unpleasantness of the dissecting room, and the dryness of the early study of anatomy which repelled him, but still more the low education and tastes of those with whom he was associated. He attributes this effect to "the absurd system of apprenticeship to an apothecary, which custom formerly, and since that an Act of Parliament, has imposed on what are called general practitioners." As so many persons now dwell on the advantages which, no doubt, the old system of apprenticeship had, we may perhaps think it worth notice that this supreme authority thought that system, viewed generally, an absurd one, and attributed to it a most evil influence on the culture of the youths entering on the study of the profession.

But whether he liked his work and its surroundings or no, Brodie was too wise, and had too well-disciplined a mind, not to do it with all his might. As he tells us, he had always been used to work hard, and now that he was working for the object of his life, he worked harder. He considered these years, 1799–1803, as the most important in his life. In a letter written to his elder son, on the occasion of his 16th birthday, he says : "When I look back at my own younger days, I feel sensible that the four years which elapsed between the ages of sixteen and twenty, were among the most valuable, if not actually the most valuable, years of my whole life. It was in that interval of time that I acquired habits of perseverance and industry, and that I learned to direct my attention to a particular object, instead of travelling from one subject to another. I think too that I can recollect my having then, for the first time, meditated on my own character, and become sensible of some of my own faults, a branch of knowledge of more consequence than all the Greek and Mathematics that schools and colleges can teach to the most zealous student. It is said to be desirable that you should know the world ; but it is much more so that you should know yourself. Always keep before your mind the maxim which was inscribed over the Temple of Delphi : Γνῶθι σεαυτόν. Those who fail to do so believe themselves to have faculties which God has not given them, or with which they are endowed only in a slight degree, while they overlook those which they really possess, and which they might cultivate with advantage. They also overlook their own faults, until these ill weeds get too strong to be rooted out, spoiling the growth of their better qualities. They are uncharitable to others because they observe their failings without being at the same time sensible that they themselves have kindred failings of their own. So there is an end of my sermon or lecture, whichever you please to call it, and which I give you not because I think you want it more than other boys, but because I think it must be useful to any boy who has just completed his sixteenth year, to have his memory jogged as to the importance of self-study and self-knowledge."

He even found companions fit for him, though few, among the members of Abernethy's class, with whom he was studying anatomy. Two he especially mentions—one died early, and is now only a name—the other was William Lawrence, the only surgeon of that day who could be placed in the same rank with Astley Cooper and Brodie, and who, in the judgment of those who knew him was, as far as mental power goes, worthy of that rank, though he never attained the public success of either of his great contemporaries. It is refreshing to read the warm eulogy which Brodie bestows on the friend of his youth, and the rival of his maturer years. It evidently springs from his heart, and it shows that that heart was as generous and as free from the baseness of envy as a great man's heart should be. Lawrence long survived Brodie, and was in active service at St. Bartholomew's Hospital till he was past 80 years of age, "still performing his duties," says Mr. Charles Hawkins (after Brodie's death), "with little less vigour than when he was first attached to that school, more than half a century ago."

It was in the autumn of 1801, at the age of 18, that Brodie came to London, and joined Abernethy's school of anatomy. In the following year he attended Mr. Wilson's lectures in Great Windmill Street and worked hard in his dissecting room ; and he now attended occasionally at the shop of a chemist and apothecary "to gain some knowledge of the Materia

Medica, and the making up of prescriptions." He makes some shrewd reflections on this gentleman's practice. "Mr. Clifton's treatment of diseases seemed to be very simple. He had in his shop five large bottles . . . and it seemed to me that out of these five bottles he prescribed for two-thirds of his patients. I do not however set this down to his discredit, for I have observed that while young members of the medical profession generally deal in a great variety of remedies, they generally discard the greater number of them as they grow older, until at last their treatment of diseases becomes almost as simple as that of the Æsculapius of Little Newport Street. There are some indeed who form an exception to this general rule, who, even to the last, seem to think that they have, or ought to have, a specific for everything, and are always making experiments with new remedies. The consequence is that they do not cure their patients, which the patients at last find out, and then they have no patients left."

Brodie's strong common sense, in fact, soon led him to anticipate, as he afterwards followed, that simplicity in prescribing medicines, which is one of the many improvements in the modern art of physic.

Nearly two years were passed in these preliminary studies before he entered in 1803 at St. George's Hospital, as a pupil of Mr. Everard Home, according to the custom of older days, when students were not so much the pupils of the hospital as of individual medical officers—a necessary consequence of the fact that there were then no organised schools officered by the whole staff of the hospital, and no proper arrangement by which the whole staff should take part in the clinical teaching. It was an effort to introduce a sounder system into hospital teaching—one more like that of our days—which originated the miserable squabble that proved fatal to John Hunter.[1]

This period of preliminary study was however by no means given up entirely to anatomy and pharmacy. Brodie had one of the most acute of minds—his interests were varied and his tastes sound—he had as we have seen unusual opportunities for entering into good and intellectual society, and still more unusual talents for making the most of those opportunities. Accordingly we find in his list of friends and associates the names of many of the leading men of a former age, Merivale, Stoddart, Gifford, Dr. Maton, Lord Glenelg, Bowdler, Francis Horner, Dr. Bateman, Sir H. Ellis, Lord Campbell, &c. And his studies show a wide range, from metaphysics (in which his favourite author seems to have been Berkeley), and the Latin classics, to the novels of the day. This extensive interest in literature and science was no bad training for one who was afterwards to preside over the Royal Society. It led him soon afterwards " to make a short essay " in periodical writing—but though some of his papers were accepted and published, he never cared to apply for the money the editor owed him, but finding that he could not well follow two trades at the same time, wisely put a stop to his literary adventures.

This period of his life was one of happy activity, of

[1] See Hunter's Life by Stephen Paget, pp. 200–219.

continued and various study, of gradual progress in the
knowledge of his profession and of increasing interest
and satisfaction in it.   First, he joined a literary club
presided over by his friend Dr. Maton, and called the
Academical Society.   This was an offspring or con-
tinuation of one originally started at Oxford, the
objects of which were innocent enough, and one of
whose rules was to exclude all questions connected
with religion and politics.   But in those days when
the French Revolution was going on, and parties were
reckless and violent at home, it excited the jealousy of
the authorities at the University, who insisted on its
being put an end to.   At these meetings, and in the
society of the talented persons, some of whom are above
enumerated, Brodie learned not only to pursue the
metaphysical and scientific subjects to which his tastes
and disposition led him,[1] but also to hold his own in
debate, and to speak in public—though his junior
standing, and the shyness which his retired mode of
living had fostered, prevented him from mixing much
in debate, and caused his speeches, as he tells us, to
have little to recommend them except their brevity.

At this early period, then, as throughout his life,
though he was working hard at his profession, he
found leisure to think of other things.   The Academical Society however did not long maintain its purity
from contentious questions, politics were gradually
introduced, and the meetings became more and more
those of an ordinary debating club.   Dr. Maton resigned his presidency after a vain attempt to enforce

[1] See Appendix B, Brodie's early metaphysical speculations.

34

the original rules, and Brodie seems to have discontinued his attendance.

In the meantime he had been more and more active in his hospital work. The commencement of these practical studies was, he tells us, a completely new era in his life. The preliminary sciences, anatomy, chemistry, etc., had evidently been followed with diligence, but more from a sense of duty than from the pleasure they gave him. Dr. Baillie had wisely advised him to make himself a tolerably complete anatomist before commencing his hospital studies. He had the wisdom to follow this advice, and had so far progressed in anatomy that he was soon afterwards able to replace the gentleman (Mr. Thomas) who was Mr. Wilson's regular demonstrator, but who was a good deal engaged in private practice and frequently did not attend ; and thus he began to superintend the pupils' studies. Before this period however he was hard at work at the hospital. His studies were interrupted by an attack of fever by which he was seized while enjoying a vacation at his father's house in 1803 and which prevented him from presenting himself at Windmill Street on October 1st when (as is still the custom of our medical schools) lectures were resumed. This illness had however one compensation, that it enabled him to know his father better, and to form both a more affectionate and a truer estimate of his character than he had been able to do when a boy. It was the last opportunity he was ever to have—for Mr. Brodie died early in the following year. He had not allowed his two sons in London to be informed of his failing health, as he did not wish to interrupt their studies, and the end came suddenly, before they could be told that he was in imminent danger. Mrs. Brodie was left with somewhat straitened means, as she was dependent on a fixed income; and in those days of high prices, war-taxation, and depreciation of paper currency though "the possessors of real property were flourishing; the incomes of professional persons kept pace with the times; and the proprietors of Bank of England stock shared large profits at the expense of the community in the shape of frequent *bonuses*; persons of fixed incomes were sadly straitened." Still Mrs. Brodie would not interrupt the career of her sons, and managed to keep up their supplies by saving all she could out of her income and not hesitating to sink a portion of her capital. We may be sure that the young men did all that was possible by their frugality to make their mother's sacrifices as little as might be.

Now comes the period of Brodie's rise at the hospital. He was, even thus early, making the acquaintance of some whose names will ever be held in remembrance at St. George's, Mr. Rose, Mr. Jeffreys, and Mr. R. Keate, and was evidently reflecting on the defects of the system then in vogue, and preparing the means of introducing one more efficient, when he should have the necessary authority. This could only be a question of time—for a man so competent, so industrious, and so well connected, could not fail to secure admission in due time on to the staff of the hospital.

The hospital system of that day was in truth very imperfect. The students were **pupils** of the individual surgeons (we hear but little of the physicians) and, when the masters were punctual and interested in teaching, their pupils got what they paid for. **This** was the case **as the** Autobiography tells us with Everard Home in the early period of his career, while his senior colleague, **Mr.** Thomas **Keate,** though **not** at all **Home's** inferior **as a surgeon, and as** Brodie thought his superior **in the medical treament** of his **patients, was so occupied in other things** that he **became negligent of his** hospital duties ; **and** of course his pupils must **have** suffered. **The** same became the case at a later period with Sir Everard Home. There was at that time no medical school, the pressure exercised by whose students and teachers (the latter **his** hospital colleagues) **must** tend to keep the most negligent **decently regular, at least,** in the discharge of his duty—no watchful **Board of Governors certain to hear** very soon of any irregularity, and to inquire **sharply** into its **cause. Nor was the** work itself **pursued with** the method and thoroughness of **modern times.** Brodie tells us that it was **from Jeffreys who preceded him as** house-surgeon that **he first** learned the importance of keeping written **notes of** cases—a practice which **he** sedulously followed **all** his life. These notes **he preserved, and** he tells us that, at the advanced period of his professional life when he wrote his Autobiography, he still often referred to them with advantage, while **Mr.** Charles Hawkins adds that **during** the winter before his death, when he was too blind to read

37

or write, these notes were read over to him by Dr. Reginald Thompson, and he dictated many observations on their contents, which are published in his collected works [1] (vol. iii. pp. 614–end). On Mr. Jeffreys vacating the house-surgeoncy, Brodie succeeded him, but only held the office from May to November, 1805, when he resigned it to undertake that of teacher in anatomy at the Windmill Street School. We may recollect that Brodie's great predecessor, John Hunter, also held the house-surgeoncy at St. George's for five months only, and then resigned it, to teach anatomy.

We may well believe that this first experience of real practice on his own account was a period of unmixed happiness for him. The position of a house surgeon is indeed one of the most agreeable modes of introduction to the actual work of the profession. There is a good deal of real responsibility—one has constantly to act on one's own motion ; and yet there is always at hand recourse to more experienced direction, and any errors that may be made are pointed out (with consideration and kind allowance, if the superior is wise) and serve as the most useful of all education. Nor, in ordinary circumstances, can such errors entail any fatal consequences to the patient, since the house surgeon is under instructions always to send for his senior in any grave emergency.

In giving his account of this part of his life, Brodie interrupts the narrative with a digression on the subject

[1] See Appendix C, Brodie on Surgical note-taking.

of lectures—a digression which has lost none of its
appropriateness during the long interval which has
elapsed since he wrote. He attended lectures, he says,
on anatomy; and during one season Dr. Crichton's [1]
lectures on the Practice of Physic, Materia Medica
and Chemistry. He entered to Mr. Abernethy's
lectures on Surgery, but too early in his career to
understand them, and attended year after year Home's
course of twelve lectures on Surgery, which he
found excellent, and from which he derived great
advantage; but his time was chiefly spent "in acquiring knowledge in other ways—and much more
substantial knowledge than can be acquired from such
dull and humdrum discourses as lectures usually are,
and what is better still I had leisure to make my own
observations, to think and reflect. Nor was this style
of education peculiar to myself. Mr. Abernethy
complained that Lawrence would not attend lectures.
My friends and contemporaries Jeffreys and Lawrence [2]
took the same course; and so it had been with
Nicolson who was some few years in advance of us.
I can easily conceive that if I had been obliged to sit
on the benches of a theatre four or five hours daily, or
tempted to compete for prizes as students are, and to
get crammed for various examinations, my position in
life afterwards would have been very different from
what it has been in reality." [3]

The question how best to train the average mind

---

[1] Afterwards Sir A. Crichton, Physician to the Emperor of Russia.
[2] I suspect this is a slip of the pen for "Rose."
[3] For Brodie's opinion of the Prize System, see Appendix D.

in the science and art of medicine is a grave one—it has become since those days a graver, and every year increases in gravity. That students are too much *taught* in these days and *learn* too little, that they are encouraged to rely too much on demonstrations and cramming, and especially that there are too many examinations, and these have too little bearing on practice, are frequent complaints. And it cannot be denied that there is at any rate some foundation for them. And if the evil existed in Brodie's student days, when the diploma of the College of Surgeons was obtained by passing a single examination of one hour, *vivâ voce* only, in anatomy and surgery exclusively, how much must it have increased now, when the subjects considered necessary have multiplied so much, and the examinations necessary—or thought necessary—to test the students' knowledge of those subjects are so numerous that it is really difficult to remember, or even to ascertain, how many they are! Let us not forget that to fail in any of these numerous trials involves mortification to the unhappy youth, and loss of time ; it involves also loss of money and bitter regret to his parents ; and besides these obvious drawbacks it involves what is, I think, a still more regrettable consequence, viz., some deterioration of the character of the rejected candidate.

When I was young, examinations were less common, and they may have been less severe, but at any rate it was much less common to be rejected, and it was thought a distinct disgrace. Now it has become so common to be plucked that it is hardly felt even as a discredit, and this results in a loss of that sensitiveness to failure or disgrace, which is at the root of manly self-reliance.

Yet while fully admitting that our students are now over "coached" and over examined; that much of their time is spent in "getting up" things that they care nothing about, and which they forget as soon as they have served their temporary purpose, we must not hide from ourselves the complexity of the problem. Great men like Brodie and Lawrence can be trusted to strain every nerve in reaching forward towards the goal of their honourable ambition, and their own innate power may be trusted to carry them thither far ahead of their commonplace contemporaries. But for the average student, who only goes into the profession because he has been told to do so, and whose ambition is limited to the humble wish to do as little as he can, and enjoy himself as much as possible, who neither loves work nor much knows how to set about it to any purpose, regulations must be made—a definite curriculum must be laid down if they are to be kept in the path at all; and as far as I see frequent daily attendances must be insisted on. Now lectures at any rate secure this, and even if they are not the best form of study, they are at least better than absolute idleness. Yet I quite believe that they are too numerous, and I also believe that the study both of anatomy and physiology is in these days too much neglected. The student hardly enters the dissecting room after he has passed the primary examinations, and physiology is not even mentioned among the

topics of the pass examination, in which surgical and
medical anatomy still finds a place. However, the
attention of the General Medical Council has been
seriously called to our system of examinations by some
of its most influential members, and we may therefore
hope that all practicable reforms will be introduced into
it. The methods of teaching must of necessity follow
those of examination.

The termination of his house-surgeoncy ended
Brodie's student days. Our next chapter will show
him starting in practice for himself, and commencing
that career which led him to wealth, to distinction,
and to as much happiness probably as this world can
give.

II

1805–1809

Early Professional Life

Assists Home in his private practice and at the College of Surgeons—
Mr. Clift—Introduction to Sir Joseph Banks—Appointed to assist
Home and Gunning at St. George's Hospital—Work in the wards
and with the students—Mr. R. Keate—First steps towards the
formation of a hospital-school—Lectures on Surgery at Wilson's
school, and on anatomy—Brodie as a reviewer.

Πρήξης αἰσχρόν ποτε μήτε μετ' ἄλλου
Μήτ' ἰδίῃ · πάντων δὲ μάλιστ' αἰσχύνεο σαυτόν
Pythagoras, Carm. Aur.
(Motto of Introductory Address. 1843).

A S soon as he gave up his office as house surgeon
at St. George's, in order to become teacher of
anatomy at the Windmill Street School, Brodie experienced the first piece of good fortune, which set
him on the road to professional success. This came in
the form of a proposal from Mr. Home to act as his
assistant in his private practice, his former assistant,
Nicolson, having received an appointment in India.
The offer was gladly accepted, accompanied as it was
by the stipulation that Home was to have his young
colleague's assistance also in his researches in compa-

43

rative anatomy. " These occupations," says Brodie, " afforded me the means of learning much as to my profession which cannot well be learnt in a hospital ; and further, by initiating me in the study of anatomy and physiology generally, without limiting my views merely to that which is required for surgical practice, they led me to scientific inquiries, which for many years afterwards formed a most agreeable addition to the drudgery of my every-day duties."

He did not get much in actual money payment out of Home's practice, for Home, though he was making an income which even now would be considered large, and which was larger then, when the value of money was so much greater than now, "had a large family and lived expensively and had nothing to spare for others." Brodie, however, expresses no dissatisfaction with the bargain, the terms of which were no doubt perfectly understood between them, and he says that with what he gained from this source, and from teaching anatomy, he began to be able to spare to some extent his mother's slender resources. So he continued for the space of two years and a half the same way of life, living in lodgings in Sackville Street, working hard in the dissecting room and the hospital, assisting Home in his private practice, taking what little practice fell in his way from such patients as would put up with the services of the junior when his senior was away for his holidays, and above all working for Mr. Home at the museum of the College of Surgeons.

The latter employment was of critical importance

for Brodie in several ways—chiefly because it obliged
him to work at scientific subjects, and thus prevented
a too exclusive devotion to the pursuit of practical
surgery. We cannot be wrong in attributing to this
cause mainly his connection with the Royal Society,
and the manysidedness of his intellectual activities.
In the first place, his work at the College Museum
brought him into intimate connection with its conservator, Mr. Clift, who having, when a boy, been taken
by John Hunter to live in his house, that he might be
trained to make drawings for him and look after his
Museum, was retained by Hunter's executors as cus-
todian of the collection, whilst its destination was
uncertain. Afterwards, when it had become the
property of the nation, and was given into the custody
of the College of Surgeons, Clift was appointed its
first conservator. The whole scientific world owes a
deep debt of gratitude to Mr. Clift for the loving care
with which he watched over the Hunterian Museum
in its early days, for the skill with which he preserved
those inestimable preparations which were made by
Hunter's own hands, and for the industry with which
he deciphered, copied and put into shape Hunter's
rough notes, and thus to a great extent repaired the
damage caused by Home's destruction of his brother-
in-law's manuscripts. To Mr. Clift also we are
indebted for the chief part of the original catalogue
of the Museum.

It was also in connection with the work he was
doing at the College that Mr. Home introduced
Brodie to Sir Joseph Banks, by whom he was re-

ceived with much cordiality, "partly from Home's recommendation and partly from knowing that I was occupied with him in making dissections in comparative anatomy"—a subject of peculiar interest to Banks. At the time of Brodie's introduction to him, Banks had long been President of the Royal Society, an office which he held fron 1778 to 1820, and he was acquainted with all the foreign as well as English men of science of the day; though in that time of war foreigners were, of course, scarce in London. He evidently took a great liking to the young surgeon and anatomist, and Brodie speaks with pleasure and evident pride of the attentions which the distinguished President showed him. He was admitted to the Sunday tea-parties which assembled at Banks's house in town—at which "everything was conducted in the plainest manner," and no other refreshment than tea was served—but at which a brilliant society congregated — "the elder Herschel, Davy, Wollaston, Young, Hatchett, Wilkins the Sanscrit scholar, Marsden, Major Rennell, Henry Cavendish, Home, Barrow, Maskelyne, Blagden, Abernethy, Carlisle, and others who have long since passed away, but whose reputation still remains, and gives a character to the age in which they lived." He was also a guest at Sir Joseph's table, and his visitor at his suburban villa at Spring Grove, which has given its name to the present suburb near Isleworth. Brodie seems to have felt a real attachment for his distinguished predecessor in the chair of the Royal Society, and gives a very pleasing idea of his simplicity and devotion to science, and to the interests of the great Society over which he so long presided.[1]

In March, 1808, Brodie made another great step forwards in the profession. Mr. Home was getting weary of the routine of hospital practice, and was glad to apply to the Governors of the hospital to appoint an assistant to relieve him of part of the charge of his patients, and as Home's application was supported by his colleague, Mr. Thomas Keate, Brodie was appointed as assistant-surgeon at the early age of not quite twenty-five. He himself describes his appointment as that of assistant-surgeon to the hospital, and no doubt it was so in the essential particular that it placed him on the staff of the hospital and gave him a claim, provided he discharged his duty satisfactorily, to promotion to the full staff when there was a vacancy. But there was a considerable difference between these assistant appointments at that time, when there were no out-patients (except those who were completing the cure which had been commenced in the wards), and those which are made at the present day, when the assistant-physician or surgeon is mainly occupied in attending to the out-patients. The difference consists in this, that the old assistants were specially appointed to assist individual members of the full staff in the care of their in-patients; so that Brodie was appointed as Home's assistant; and Dr. Page in the interesting and comprehensive account which he gives of the Hospital in the first volume of

[1] Sir Humphry Davy, in his will, left Brodie £50 to be laid out in a token of remembrance.

"The St. George's Hospital Reports" does not classify any one as assistant-surgeon before Mr. Babington, who was appointed to that office in 1829, and who was, in Dr. Page's view, the first assistant-surgeon to the hospital, Dr. Hope having been elected as the first assistant-physician in 1834. So comparatively recent is the growth of that out-patient system which now lies like an incubus on all our London hospitals.

Brodie had at this time no regular private practice; he had not even thought it worth while to put his name on his street door, so that he had ample leisure for hospital work. His work there was soon increased by the departure of the junior surgeon, Mr. Gunning, to the Peninsular War. Mr. Gunning had an old connection with the army, and with St. George's Hospital, for his uncle had been Surgeon-General to the army and was surgeon to St. George's Hospital for over thirty years. He himself (as he told me when I met him, then in extreme old age, at Paris) had walked by the side of Hunter's coach as it carried home his dead body from St. George's Hospital. He had then served with the Duke of York's army in Flanders in 1793-4, and was, like his uncle, Surgeon-in-Chief to the army. There could hardly be said at that time to be a regular army medical service, and the weekly Board at St. George's were empowered to grant unlimited leave of absence to any of their surgeons who might be abroad with the army. Such leave was granted to Mr. Gunning, when he left England to join Sir Arthur Wellesley's army in the

Peninsula,[1] from which service he did not return till the conclusion of the war. During his absence his patients were placed under the care of Mr. R. Keate (who was his uncle's assistant) and Brodie jointly. As Home interfered very little in the management of those who were nominally his patients at the hospital, and as Brodie had both leisure and zeal in abundance, he threw himself with ardour into his hospital work, passing "several hours daily in the wards, taking notes of cases and communicating freely with the students." This was during the six months in which the dissecting room was closed, and even during the other six months he spent in the hospital wards all the time he could spare from teaching anatomy. This constant attendance at the hospital was an immense improvement, in the interests both of the patients and the students, on the practice of all the Metropolitan hospitals of that day. For at that time the surgeons used only to go round the wards on two days in the week, and never attend otherwise, except when there were operations to perform, or when they were specially sent for on emergencies. Brodie and Mr. R. Keate were the first persons to adopt a different method. They were at their posts daily, and superintended everything, and there was never an urgent case which they did not visit in the evening, and not unfrequently early in the morning also. No wonder that the effect of so

---

[1] "Mr. Gunning being ordered abroad on His Majesty's service, requested leave of absence from the hospital—the other surgeons undertaking to do his hospital duty during his absence—granted."—"Minutes of Weekly Board," June 15, 1808.

healthy a change was soon visible "in the increase of zeal and diligence on the part of the students and in their increasing numbers." It was, in fact, the commencement of Brodie's reputation as a surgeon and a teacher of surgery, and of the rise of the St. George's school to the high position which it held during the whole period of Brodie's service there.

Another improvement of great importance for the teaching of surgery was introduced by Brodie about this time, in the appointment of clinical clerks, one for Home's patients, and another for those of Mr. Gunning who were under his care. This was a happy innovation, for surgeons require careful notes of their cases no less than physicians do, and surgical cases present daily changes and fluctuations, the accurate observation of which is as necessary to their successful treatment, as is that of the medical cases. It was no doubt Brodie's more literary and more scientific way of looking at surgery which led him to introduce this more thorough method of pursuing its study ; and the same cause also led him at this period to begin a course of clinical lectures on surgery, "the first lectures of this kind, as I believe," he says, "which were ever delivered in a London hospital." Those who have read the painful account of the quarrel between John Hunter and his colleagues at St. George's will recollect that the essential point in dispute was this : they wished the students' fees to form a common fund, but without being willing (no doubt because some of them at least felt themselves unable) to teach surgery clinically ; while Hunter contended that he was entitled to the fees paid by the students (many of them his Scotch compatriots) who came to enrol themselves under him ; or that if the fund was to be common all the surgeons ought to bear their share in the clinical teaching in common. It was this common teaching by all the staff of the hospital, which was the ultimate and necessary end towards which the clinical lectures introduced by Brodie tended. They were soon afterwards taken up by his colleagues and successors, and they have now become part of the regular duties of all hospital physicians and surgeons. Thus the idea of common teaching by the whole hospital staff, which Hunter suggested, has become the model of all hospital schools. It is greatly to the credit of St. George's, and still more to that of Brodie, that he was the first to introduce a practice so rational, and in fact so necessary.

In some of these improvements in hospital practice and teaching Brodie, as we have seen, had the concurrence of Mr. Robert Keate, his slightly older colleague,[1] to whom Brodie pays in his Autobiography a warm and even affectionate tribute ; and this he has also repeated in public in an address which he gave in distributing the prizes at St. George's Hospital in 1850 (vol. i. 533 [2]). Mr. Keate was at that time assistant at the hospital to his uncle, Thomas Keate, whom he also assisted

---

[1] Keate was born in 1777, and died in 1857.

[2] N.B.—All references, in this form, throughout the book, are to Brodie's Collected Works in 3 vols., edited by Mr. Charles Hawkins, 1865.

in his office of Surgeon-General to the Army (an office which John Hunter had held before him), and was introduced by him to the notice of the Royal Family, with whom he became a great favourite, attended many of them privately, and served as Serjeant Surgeon to King William IV. and to the present Queen. He preceded Brodie as surgeon to the hospital, having been appointed in 1813, when his uncle resigned,[1] and he retained his office for many years after Brodie's resignation, and in fact for some time after he had ceased to perform its duties. The abuse, in his and other cases, of hospitals being nominally officered by old men who had ceased in fact to perform their duties, and who, of course, could do nothing for the instruction of students, led to the salutary limitations as to age and tenure of office which are now, I believe, in force at all hospitals, at least in London. If, however, Mr. Keate erred in clinging too long to office, we may remember that he had great example, as well as the inevitable tendency of age, to excuse his error, and we, who knew but little of him personally, may well accept the testimony of one who knew him so long and so intimately to this effect : "He was a perfect gentleman, in every sense of the word ; kind in his feelings ; open, honest, and upright in his conduct. His professional knowledge and his general character made him a most useful officer of the hospital ; and now that our *game has been played*, it is with great satisfaction that I look back to the

---

[1] The elder Keate died in 1821.

long and disinterested friendship that existed between us."

Now began the first tentative efforts to found a regular school, for up to this time, though famous men had taught physic, surgery, and anatomy in London, and some of them in more especial connection with certain hospitals, it could hardly be said that there was anything which deserved the name of a hospital school, or in fact was so regarded. Thus when Pott taught surgery at St. Bartholomew's, or John Hunter at St. George's, or Abernethy anatomy at St. Bartholomew's, their lectures were attended by scholars from all parts of London, and doubtless by many who had no connection with any school whatever. Hunter attended Pott's lectures, as Brodie did the anatomical lectures of Abernethy, without any reference to the school of St. Bartholomew's. In fact, there was then no school of that hospital apart from the lectures of eminent persons which might be delivered within its precincts for the lecturer's convenience; while other lecturers, *e.g.*, William Hunter and James Wilson, equally for their own convenience, lectured in private premises, as a private speculation. Brodie's lectures on surgery were commenced in this semi-private way, when in 1808 he joined with Wilson in the delivery of a course of surgical lectures in the Windmill Street School; and it was not till long afterwards that the school was moved to the neighbourhood of St. George's Hospital, and its pupils received their whole medical education in the wards of that hospital. Wilson did not long continue to lecture on surgery,[1] and Brodie remained in sole possession of that department, lecturing to the pupils of the Windmill Street School and Mr. Brookes's Anatomical School in Blenheim Street till twenty years afterwards, when he resigned the lectures to Mr. Babington and Mr. Cæsar Hawkins. Brodie tells us that his lectures were very popular, though he modestly adds that his stock of knowledge was at first limited, and his delivery for many years constrained and awkward. The cause which he assigns for that success was no doubt the true one—the same, in fact, which has been the secret of the success of all really great teachers, viz., that " whatever information he gave was drawn from or confirmed by his own observation, and that he was really in earnest in his endeavours to instruct his pupils." Still he did not neglect books ; his lectures were carefully composed, illustrated by analyses of his MS. notes of cases, and his opinions compared with the results arrived at by the most recent surgical writers. At first he wrote out his lectures in full, but soon contented himself with pretty full notes, which he then abridged for use in the theatre. In fact, written lectures are a mistake, when addressed to an audience so volatile and so prone to fun and mischief as our medical students are. It is impossible to hold their

[1] Dr. Wilson always maintained that his father founded these lectures for Brodie's especial benefit, partly from friendship for the young man himself, and partly out of gratitude to Dr. Baillie, with whom Brodie was so nearly connected.

attention if your eyes are fixed on your manuscript. You must look at them and address yourself directly to them if they are to listen to what you say. And indeed some of the most effective lectures I have ever heard were delivered by an eloquent professor at Rome, walking up and down a circular area, and speaking particularly now to one, now to another group of listeners, as his Roman ancestors used to pace up and down the Rostra while haranguing the crowd in the Forum. Brodie had keen eyes and a very expressive face (as may be seen in his portrait), and no doubt made good use of both voice and expression in addressing his class, instead of mumbling out of a manuscript.

Then came a period when Wilson, who was now very busy in private practice, called upon him to take a part of the anatomical lectures ; for hitherto he seems only to have acted as demonstrator in the anatomical school. This involved severe labour indeed. In those days, when there were no railways, omnibuses, or even cabs, when London was relatively small, and the suburbs by no means easy or at night safe of access, all men lived near their place of business. Students consequently were always on the spot, and therefore the lecturers lectured in the evening, so as to leave the day free for practice. Brodie tells us that, having a pretty large acquaintance, he was almost always out at dinner on days when he had no evening lecture, and then had to get home early to arrange the lectures for next day—a task which often lasted till three or four in the morning.

So passed away a period of about a year and a half
after his election as assistant surgeon at St. George's.
He did not put his name on the door, but lived in his
lodgings, busy with his lectures, his hospital practice,
his duties as assistant to Home in his private practice,
and his work at the College Museum with Home
and Clift in comparative anatomy. He had, as he
says, nothing that deserved the name of private
practice, but his life was one of great occupation,
as we can easily believe from the above account of
it. It is to this period that an abortive attempt to
found a medical periodical under the title of the
Annual Medical Review and Register belongs. It
was started by Dr. Bateman, who asked Brodie to
join with himself and Dr. Henderson in its management. He declined, but wrote for it a few reviews
of books, such as Hooper's "Anatomist's Vade
Mecum," Cooper's "Surgical Dictionary," and
"Allan on Lithotomy." The periodical was a
failure, and Brodie speaks of it in somewhat slight-
ing and contemptuous terms, saying: "I have
looked back on it since as a very foolish concern,
in which it would have been much wiser for me
never to have interfered. I need scarcely add
that I have never repeated the mistake or written
another medical review." One hardly sees the
reason for this severity, or why he should say that
he had not "sufficient practical knowledge to be
qualified to do justice to such an undertaking."
Surely a man who held Brodie's position and had
his experience of anatomical schools and hospitals

was eminently fitted, apart from personal qualities, to judge of the three books above mentioned, and we should be happy to be able to think that all reviewers of the present day had as much experience.[1] But the incident is worth noting, as showing his severe judgment of his own work, and perhaps also the contempt with which practical men are apt to regard literature in general and periodical literature in particular.

So far Brodie can hardly be said to have even seriously attempted private practice. He had hitherto, and very wisely, considering his age, contented himself with laying a sure foundation in the esteem of some amongst the most eminent men of the day, and in the profound knowledge of his profession which years of hard work could not fail to bring to a mind like his. We shall now find him established in a house of his own, and making rapid strides on the way which leads upwards to the summit of the surgical profession.

[1] See Appendix E, Brodie as a medical reviewer.

III

1809–1816

EARLY DAYS OF PRACTICE

Takes a house and pupils—His contemporaries, Keate and Lawrence—
Elected F.R.S.—Wins the Copley Medal—Scientific societies—
Treatise on Diseases of the Joints—Ceases to lecture on Anatomy—
Life in Society. Holland House—Overwork and illness—End of
the great war—Foreign visitors to London.

> " To catch Dame Fortune's golden smile,
> Assiduous wait upon her ;
> And gather gear by every wile
> That's justified by Honour ;
> Not for to hide it in a hedge,
> Not for a train attendant,
> But for the glorious privilege
> Of being independent."
>
> BURNS.

IT was in the autumn of 1809 that Brodie first
ventured to take a house, and " set up in practice." This was four years after his service as house
surgeon at St. George's. He was then only 26 years
of age. This interval between the time when his
student career was technically over, and that at which
he began the serious search for private practice, was

58

anything but wasted. During the greater part of that interval he had been discharging the functions, though without the formal title, of Surgeon to the Hospital ; and had thus learned surgery in the only school in which it can be learned—that is by practice. He had made a good name for himself as a clinical teacher, and had won fame and acceptance as a lecturer, both on anatomy and surgery. And beside these professional advantages, which his industry and originality had won for him (for in those days it was an original idea to seek for practice by the noble method of reforming the service of his hospital), he had taken a high place in scientific circles, and was evidently marked out as one of the likeliest men to lead the surgical profession ; for though Lawrence and Keate were his competitors, and both were men of great ability, yet Keate was evidently inferior to Brodie in everything except influence and connection ; and in England, at least, though Court influence is valuable, it can never outweigh public and scientific reputation ; while Lawrence, though of supreme ability, and in some respects perhaps even Brodie's superior, yet had not the *savoir vivre* which distinguished the latter. Lawrence indeed always gave one the impression of a man who from some spiritual defect could not attain to the height which nature had intended for him, as far as his intellect was concerned. We have seen, however, how far Brodie was from regarding these competitors with either envy or malice. He had the cheerful confidence in himself which his talents and energy justified ; was determined to make

the best of his great abilities, and contented to take
what fortune might have in store for him, without
grumbling if others should be more highly favoured.
At present his fortunes were certainly not high, for he
tells us that he could not have furnished his house if
his mother had not advanced him the money. But
this seems to have been the last call he had to make
on her affection and self-sacrifice. He took pupils
into his house (22, Sackville Street), and thereby
balanced the extra expenditure of housekeeping. His
income from lecturing increased, and private practice
began to come in, so that he made between £200 and
£300 from this source in his first year. He was
never, he says, in debt, and had always money in
hand.

Relieved thus from pecuniary anxieties, he was able
to apply himself to the scientific researches which he
loved. The works of Bichat, which were then
recent, directed his attention to physiological subjects ;
but he had previously communicated to the Royal
Society a paper, on the Dissection of a Fœtus which
had no Heart, of which he himself speaks as "of little
or rather of no value," but which at any rate gained
him admission as a F.R.S. in March, 1810, and in
November of the same year he delivered the Croonian
Lecture, "On the Influence of the Brain on the
action of the Heart, and the Generation of Animal
Heat," and also communicated a paper on "The
effects produced by certain Vegetable Poisons."
These papers produced so favourable an impression
that the Council awarded to him the Copley Medal

in the autumn of 1811. The only objection made to this award was by one of the Councillors, who observed that the medal had never before been given to so young a man; to which Wollaston made the very proper reply that if the medal was deserved (which no one seems to have contested), the author's youth was an additional reason why he should have it. Brodie dwells with pride and pleasure on the gratification which this rapid success gave him, and on the happiness which he felt in this early period of his life, when the prospects of coming fame and fortune were becoming visibly brighter and brighter: and he very properly attributes much of the success which now began to attend his professional efforts to the rank which he had thus attained in scientific circles.

This period of Brodie's life is indeed almost entirely a record of work at the Royal Society and of increasing private practice. It was on these two foundations that he was gradually erecting the edifice of his public fame and influence, which was afterwards to rise so high.

We hear of his engagements, partly convivial, partly scientific, at the "Animal Chemistry Club," which was at first a scientific society, meeting alternately at the houses of Mr. Home and Mr. Hatchett, for the discussion of chemical and scientific subjects after dinner, and which consisted, besides the two hosts and Brodie, of Davy, Dr. Babington,[1] Mr.

[1] This Dr. Babington is not to be confounded with Mr. Babington (Lord Macaulay's uncle), who was afterwards Surgeon to St. George's

Brande, Mr. Clift, Mr. Children, and Dr. Warren.
Afterwards it became a mere dining club, and Brodie
ceased to take any interest in it.

Another society which was exclusively medical,
was of more public interest. It was called the
"Society for the Promotion of Medical and Chirurgical Knowledge," and was founded by John Hunter
and Mr. Fordyce, and it was in its Transactions that
the famous proposal of John Hunter for the ligature
of the femoral artery in the treatment of popliteal
aneurism was formulated, and its application by Hunter
in his first five cases described by Sir Everard Home
(see Hunter's works, by Palmer, vol. iii.). Of this
society Brodie remained a member from 1808 till its
dissolution in 1818, by which time indeed it had
become superfluous, being superseded by the Medico-
Chirurgical Society. Brodie was elected secretary to
this Society in 1812, but it also had then become
little more than a dining club, and his office was
almost nominal. He wrote a paper for the third and
last volume of the "Transactions of the Society for the
Promotion of Medical and Chirurgical Knowledge,"

Hospital. Dr. Babington was President of the Medico-Chirurgical
Society in 1817-19, before its incorporation. He was Physician to
Guy's Hospital, having commenced his service there as Apothecary, and
he was a man of great scientific attainments, especially in mineralogy
and chemistry. He was the founder of the Geological Society, and its
president in 1822, but with the true modesty of a scholar, he took
lessons and attended lectures in both geology and chemistry after that
period. He was in active practice till four days before his death from
influenza in 1833. "History" says Dr. Munk, "does not supply us
with a physician more loved or more respected than Dr. Babington." .
His son, also physician to Guy's Hospital, was an eminent linguist.

which he characteristically describes as "of very little value." The medical reader can judge for himself. It treats of a case of abscess of the brain connected with disease of the ear, and is published as the first paper in the third volume of Brodie's works, collected by Mr. Charles Hawkins. It seems to invert the relation of cause and effect between the two things of which it treats, but no doubt at that early period the subject was a new one, and the paper had at any rate the merit of calling attention to it. If, however, we are obliged to coincide in Brodie's estimate of this early production, at least when regarded in the light of the present state of surgery, we are not the less bound to admire the rigorous censure of himself which is so attractively blended, in the Autobiography, with the warmest and most generous appreciation of his friends and contemporaries.

Amongst the latter we find at this period the record of the commencement of his life-long friendship with Mr. Brande, Sir Humphry Davy's successor in the chair of Chemistry at the Royal Institution. It was this friendship, no doubt, which procured for the older generation of students at St. George's the inestimable privilege of obtaining their chemistry lectures from Mr. Brande at Albemarle Street, a privilege of which I have heard many of them speak with the warmest gratitude.

All this scientific work, however, was not allowed to interfere with practice, for although he still pursued his physiological investigations he was chiefly occupied with the business of the hospital, taking and arranging notes of cases, and adding to the lectures on surgery whatever information he had acquired ; and the result was shown in the gratifying fact that his receipts from private practice increased at the rate of about £200 or £250 annually.

And now began his serious work on the literature of Surgery ; for it was at this period (about 1812), that he first set to work systematically at the great topic with which his name will always be associated as a surgical writer—the Diseases of Joints. He tells us that the subject had been in his mind ever since he had dissected, during the period of his house-surgeoncy, a specimen of what is called spontaneous (or pathological) dislocation of the hip, *i.e.*, the displacement of the thigh bone which follows disease of that joint. Recognising the undoubted fact that the treatment of diseases of the joints was at that time as unscientific as possible, he had always kept that department of surgery before him, as one specially in need of investigation, and had accordingly taken notes of almost every case of articular disease occurring amongst his hospital patients, ever since he became assistant surgeon ; had taken every opportunity that presented itself for dissecting any case of incipient joint disease, in post-mortem examinations of those who had died from other causes ; and had made what examinations and observations he could in the cases of patients of other medical men. But the subject was a peculiarly difficult one, since these affections do not end fatally, till the pathological changes they produce have reached an advanced stage, and disorganised the joint, while Brodie's object was to particularise their early stages, and by ascertaining their natural progress in those early stages, to infer the appropriate treatment by which that progress could be stopped. This is in fact the truly scientific surgery, which is based on pathology.

So he struggled laboriously on to the light, but it was a long and a hard labour. At the end of the first year, he says, he seemed no wiser than at the beginning, and at the end of the second he knew little more than at the end of the first. But at length some glimmering of light dawned on his studies, and he had accumulated enough knowledge to begin the preparation of the paper which is found in the fourth volume of that great storehouse of medical knowledge, the "Medico-Chirurgical Transactions." This paper was read on April 13, 1813, apparently before he had himself joined the Society, as it was communicated by Dr. Roget : and it was soon followed by another in the fifth volume of the same series.

These papers are the beginning of what is perhaps Brodie's principal contribution to practical surgery— viz., his great treatise on Diseases of the Joints. And here, if the general reader is startled and repelled by the mention of "surgery," let me call his attention to the fact that the aim of "practical surgery" is to save men's lives and limbs—an object surely of interest to every one, however remote from medicine his occupations and studies may be, and one therefore on which I may be allowed to speak briefly. Before Brodie's time, as he himself points out in the first of these papers (read in 1813), "No one had undertaken to investigate the subject with a view to make a classification of the morbid affections to which the joints are liable."[1] The consequence was that, as is stated in the same paper, "the term 'white swelling' was applied, almost indiscriminately, to all the affections to which the joints are liable."[2] Thus diseases perfectly, and even easily, curable in their origin, were mixed up with others that are possibly incurable, and so these curable affections were allowed to go on till they ended in demanding amputation, or exhausted the patient's powers and led him to a lingering death. Still worse, no one had clearly drawn the line between real diseases, or diseases accompanied by perceptible changes in the parts affected, and those mysterious maladies—possibly partly imaginary, but, for all that, most painful—which are very generally classed as "hysterical," but are perhaps better styled "neurotic," as depending on the nervous system, and which are largely influenced by mental causes. It was Brodie's chief achievement, as a surgeon, that he threw so clear a light on that most important, because most common, class of diseases which affect the joints, and it is to this chiefly that his friends and admirers must have referred, when they chose the motto for his medal from the lines of Lucretius,

"E tenebris tantis tam clarum extollere lumen,
Qui primus potuisti inlustrans commoda vitæ."[3]

---

[1] "Medico-Chirurgical Transactions," iv. 207.
[2] Ibid., p. 232, note.
[3] "De Rer. Nat.," iii. 1, 2.

The papers before us deal with the first branch of
the inquiry—viz., the classification of joint diseases,
and the indications which show what structure is
primarily or chiefly affected, and they are in the best
style of hospital work. They rest on an abundance
of cases, well described and carefully followed out to
their conclusion ; and they form the basis of the great
work, which was published five years afterwards, on
Diseases of the Joints, contained in the second volume
of his collected works, in which for the first time all
such affections are classified as are accompanied by
visible changes of structure. The local nervous affections both of joints and other parts are dealt with in
the " Lectures on Local Nervous Affections," in the
third volume, which seem to have been compiled from
his surgical lectures at St. George's. He gives here
(lect. ii.) a clear account of the steps by which he
was led to suspect the real nature of affections which
at that time had always been confounded with organic
disease, and for which amputation has been sometimes
performed,[1] whilst in many cases painful and prolonged
treatment was prescribed, and long confinement and
perfect repose enjoined, for ailments which such
regimen only aggravated. So common are these
disorders that Brodie does not " hesitate to declare
that, among the higher classes of society, at least four-
fifths of the female patients who are commonly

---

[1] See a story related by Sir Benjamin's biographer in the *Lancet*, vol. i.,
1850, p. 542. Some such cases are also referred to in Brodie's third
lecture on " Local Nervous Affections."

supposed to labour under diseases of the joints, labour under hysteria, and nothing else."

Even non-medical readers might peruse with advantage the remarks which Brodie makes on this subject.

Probably these diseases are less common now than they were then, for he points out one fertile source of such complaints amongst young ladies, and one way of diminishing their frequency, in the following words : " You can render no more essential service to the more affluent classes of society than by availing yourselves of every opportunity of explaining to those among them who are parents, how much the ordinary system of education tends to engender the disposition to these diseases among their female children. If you would go further, so as to make them understand in what their error consists, what they ought to do, and what they ought to leave undone, you need only point out the difference between the plans usually pursued in the bringing up of the two sexes. The boys are sent at an early age to school, where a large portion of their time is passed in taking exercise in the open air ; while their sisters are confined to heated rooms, taking little exercise out of doors, and often none at all except in a carriage. Then, for the most part, the latter spend more of their time in study than the former. The mind is over-educated at the expense of the physical structure, and, after all, with little advantage to the mind itself ; for who can doubt that the principal object of this part of education ought to be, not so much to fill the mind with knowledge as to train it to a right exercise of its intellectual and moral faculties, or that, other things being the same, this is more easily accomplished in those whose animal functions are preserved in a healthy state, than it is in others ? "

Young ladies have now a more natural, and more active life than they had eighty years since, and for this salutary change the great authority of Brodie can be quoted, as far as its physical aspects are concerned.

Much more would be said about these masterly surgical treatises if we were writing for professional readers only. What has been said must suffice to give some idea to the general reader how directly Brodie's surgical labours tended to benefit humanity, and to " shed a light on the true interests of life." [1]

Of his work on the joints the author says, not more modestly than truly, that his " labours have not been in vain, and that a great number of limbs are now preserved, which would in former times have been amputated as a matter of course." Solid as was this great advance in surgery, Brodie was well aware that he had only laid a foundation to be built on by those whose inquiries should begin where his terminated, and that he would thus be, as he expresses it, " left behind." But so, as he says, " it must be in all matters within the range of the physical sciences ; and if this be the case as to chemistry and physiology, much more must it be so as to so difficult a science as

[1] It is thus that Munro renders Lucretius' words " inlustrans commoda vitæ."

pathology, in the pursuit of which we get little or no help from experiments."

If, however, it be true, as no doubt it is, that eighty years of vigorous effort, and the wonderful advance which the introduction of chloroform and the labours of Lister have made in the surgical treatment of disease, have left Brodie's work to some extent behind ; yet we cannot but recollect that it was that work which first put the treatment of joint disease on the only sure footing—that of pathological fact, and sound reasoning from such fact—and that all the advance which has since been made has been made by following his method.

Another important epoch in Brodie's surgical career arrived when, in the spring of 1812, Mr. Wilson found himself obliged, by the calls of an increasing practice, to give up his occupation as a teacher of anatomy. He offered to convey his interest in the school in Great Windmill Street, together with the Museum, and the adjoining house in which he then lived, and where William Hunter, and afterwards Baillie, had resided, to Brodie, for the sum of £7,000. But Brodie, though he had acquired a good standing and considerable reputation as a lecturer on anatomy, and had a very capable colleague, Dr. Harrison, who would have willingly joined him, was unwilling to charge himself with the pecuniary liability which must have been incurred, for he had no funds of his own at his disposal. So, by the advice of Sir Everard Home and Dr. Baillie, the offer was declined. Nor did he think it fair to Mr.

Wilson, who had treated him always, he says, with much kindness, to entertain Harrison's proposal that they should set up independently as joint teachers of anatomy, since this would have seriously damaged Wilson's chance of disposing of his school, and so the result was that Sir Charles Bell purchased the Museum and took Mr. Wilson's place.

This ended Brodie's career as a lecturer on anatomy. When he wrote the Autobiography forty years afterwards, he tells us that he still retained all the anatomical knowledge required for practice, and believed then that a short time spent in the dissecting-room would have enabled him to resume his duties as a demonstrator of anatomy. But we cannot doubt that it was to his benefit as a surgeon that he was from this time relieved of the labours of the anatomical school, though, as we shall see, he did not suspend his voluntary studies in physiology.

Now followed two or three years of quiet, diligent, and successful work as a surgeon. He still acted for Home in his private practice, and assisted him in his researches in comparative anatomy, and so had ample employment for his working hours. But he did not sink into the mere professional drudge. He saw a great deal of very good society, and he speaks with especial interest and gratitude of Sir Thomas Plumer, who was then Attorney-General, and afterwards became Master of the Rolls, and whose daughter married my old friend and teacher, Mr. Cutler, who was long Brodie's assistant. Another more famous mansion at which he was intimate was Holland

House, then the home of a famous literary circle : Rogers, Sydney Smith, Allen, and later on, Macaulay. We have seen that Brodie's family had an old connection with that of Lord Holland, and this had been made closer by the fact that Marsh, who had been Lord Holland's tutor at Christ Church, and afterwards travelled with him on the Continent, and became his intimate friend, was the husband of Brodie's elder sister, and succeeded the Rev. P. B. Brodie as Rector of Winterslow. Of the occupants of Holland House, and of many distinguished persons he met there, Brodie speaks with warm appreciation ; but I find no reference to Macaulay in the Autobiography, though Brodie had as a colleague the uncle, Mr. Babington, after whom Macaulay was named. Macaulay himself was not introduced at Holland House till 1831, at which time Brodie was probably too busy to be there often. Of Lord Holland he gives a most attractive picture, as Macaulay also does, and of Lady Holland, as of almost all the persons whom he thinks it necessary to notice in the Autobiography, he also speaks kindly. In fact, he seems to have acted on the sound and good rule of not recording the names of those of whom he could not say something favourable—*nil nisi bonum.* And so the impression we get of Lady Holland from his mention of her (slight though it is) is much more favourable than that which "Macaulay's Life and Letters" conveys.[1] He says, perhaps with a little covert sarcasm, "Fortunately, I had no favours to ask

[1] See the letters dated May 30th, and July 25, 1831, in chap. iv. of " Macaulay's Life and Letters," by Sir G. O. Trevelyan.

of her or of any one else ; but during thirty years or intimate acquaintance with her, I never knew her miss an opportunity of showing me any small mark of kindness in her power."

His occupations were now interrupted by an illness which obliged him to seek a short repose by the seaside. This was in the autumn of 1814. In those days, when travelling was so laborious, about eight miles an hour the usual pace, and a journey of some seventy to eighty miles quite enough for a day, and accompanied, besides, with so many drawbacks from rough weather, bad accommodation, and high prices, it is not wonderful that the annual holiday, which we have come to look upon as almost a necessity, especially for hard-worked professional men, was only seldom enjoyed, except by those who were peculiarly favoured by circumstances. So we find in the Autobiography no trace of his having sought for rest and change in the country during all the years which had passed since his father's death.[1] But this constant labour was now so telling on his health that he became dyspeptic, lost flesh, and was so visibly ill, that many of his friends thought he must have some organic disease, and it was predicted of him that he would cause the next vacancy on the staff of St. George's. He was obliged, therefore, to take the repose which he would have prescribed to others. He went, with his

---

[1] I was once told by Mr. Charles Hawkins that at a much later period of his life, when at the height of his practice, Sir Benjamin did not leave London for eight years, except on hurried professional journeys —calls which entailed not rest, but severer work.

friend Brande, for a short stay at the seaside, and returned quite an altered person, though he suffered a slight relapse in the winter.

The great war was now coming to an end ; in fact, had stopped for the time, with Napoleon's first abdication ; and ceased with the thunder-clap of the Hundred days. Foreign medical and scientific celebrities began to flock over to England, among the former, Roux, who was for many years the principal surgeon in Paris, and who has left so graphic and so appreciative a reminiscence of his English experiences in his "Relation d'un Voyage fait à Londres en 1814,"[1] Assalini, an Italian surgeon, who had accompanied Napoleon's expeditions to Egypt and to Russia, had witnessed the burning of Moscow, and used to entertain his hearers with many tales of those stirring times,[2] Orfila, Magendie, Ekstrom of Stockholm, Wagner and others from Germany. All these were naturally attracted to Brodie as being the most rising young surgeon in London, and the most in touch with foreign men and manners. For though he seems never to have acquired the conversational use of any foreign tongue, he was a zealous student of French medical and scientific literature, and always had a mind open to receive any new idea from abroad. Amongst the famous men of science whose friendship he then made, he names Blainville and Berzelius, and records in a few words

[1] See Appendix F., Roux's Account of his Visit to London.
[2] At St. George's we have always been accustomed to use Assalini's tenaculum, and other inventions of this once celebrated surgeon, doubtless survivals of his acquaintance with Brodie.

his having met the great Humboldt, and how on one occasion Humboldt accompanied him back to the West End from Somerset House, where the Royal Society then met, and how he talked without intermission, displaying an immense store of knowledge, but passing continually from one subject to another, without any visible connection between them. "When," says Brodie, "I afterwards read that very remarkable, but rather unreadable, production of his later years, 'Cosmos,' it reminded me very forcibly of the conversation which I had with him, *or rather which he had with me*, more than thirty years previously." The words I have italicised give a neat and epigrammatic idea of the omniscient bore, and show that Brodie was not wanting in that "pawky" humour which the world has agreed to connect with the nation from which his ancestors sprang.

IV

1816-1823

MARRIAGE. PROFESSIONAL SUCCESS

Brodie's marriage with Miss Sellon—Their children—The second Sir
Benjamin Brodie—Liebig's visit to London—King's College—
Years of increasing prosperity—Some of Brodie's contemporaries,
Sir W. Knighton and Sir R. Croft—Moves to Savile Row—
Lectures at the College of Surgeons—Brodie on drowning and
asphyxia—First introduction to the Court—Appointed Surgeon to
St. George's Hospital—Dr. Matthew Baillie—Dr. Thomas Young.

"Love for the maiden crowned with marriage, no regrets for ought that
  has been,
Household happiness, gracious children, debtless competence, golden
  mean."   TENNYSON.

IN the year 1816 Brodie married a daughter of
Serjeant Sellon, a distinguished lawyer, whose
acquaintance he had made through Mr. Peter Brodie,
his eldest brother, himself then rising into repute as a
conveyancer. This marriage, like all the great events
of his life, turned out most successful—and at the
time when he wrote his Autobiography, thirty-nine
years afterwards, he could write, evidently from his
heart, of their unaltered mutual affection, and of the
happiness and content which he had derived from the
worthy character of the three children who then

survived. This worth, as he says, must have been mainly due to the care with which their mother watched over the training of their infancy and childhood, at a time when their father was far too much occupied to give them the attention which he would otherwise have bestowed. It is clear, however, that he had every reason to know that they were safe in their mother's hands, and under her loving and gentle guidance.

The children who survived to maturity were three—the second Sir Benjamin Brodie; a daughter who married the Rev. E. Hoare; and another son, the Rev. W. Brodie.

It is not within the scope of this work to give any detailed account of Brodie's eldest son, who, as is well known, became afterwards one of the most distinguished chemists of his day, but still as no life of Brodie would be complete which did not contain some mention of his family, it may not be out of place to say a few words here on this subject.

The elder of the two sons, who bore the same two names as his father, was born February 5, 1817. He was sent at the age of eight years to a school at Rottingdean, near Brighton, kept by a Dr. Hooker. This gentleman appears to have been much attached to the boy, who always spoke of him in after years with great regard.

In 1828 he was sent to Harrow, being placed in the house of the Rev. H. Drury. In 1834 he wrote that "he was head of his house, and was by reason of that dignity installed in an arm-chair at dinner, and was learning with all becoming patience the most difficult art of carving." In the same year he was awarded the Peel gold medal for Latin prose. In 1835 he wrote, "Our scholarship finished this afternoon and I am second! So give me three cheers. I have got a scholarship to Caius College, Cambridge, at my option whether to take it or not. Of course I am not to take it, but I said I would leave it in doubt till I heard from you."

Brodie was not one of those who would wish his son to avail himself of a scholarship of which he did not really stand in need, and in the autumn of the same year he went up as a commoner to Balliol. That this was a wise proceeding there can be no doubt. No one could possibly regret becoming a member of a college which then, or during the next few years contained as undergraduate members such men as Jowett, Clough, Stafford Northcote, Goulburn, the Farrers, Hobhouse, and numerous others. Many were the friends he made at Balliol, and the intimate terms on which he stood with the future Master are shown by the correspondence, some of which has been lately published in the "Life of Jowett," by E. Abbot and L. Campbell.

Whilst at Balliol young Brodie appears to have drifted from the study of classics, and in 1838 he took his B.A. degree, obtaining a second class in mathematics. After leaving Oxford he entered as a student at Lincoln's Inn, and commenced to read for the Bar in the chambers of his uncle, but this form of study was so very uncongenial to him that he soon relinquished it and turned his attention to science. He then went to Giessen to study chemistry under Liebig, whose name was attracting students from all parts of the world. On his return to England he lived in London, working in a laboratory of his own, delivering lectures at the Royal Institution, and pursuing his researches, on various kinds of wax, which had been commenced some years before on Liebig's suggestion.

In the spring of the year 1845, Liebig paid a visit to England and dined with Sir Benjamin at Savile Row. Lady Brodie wrote to her son, then working in Liebig's laboratory at Giessen, " I was most agreeably surprised in Liebig, his appearance and manner is so much more gentlemanlike, intellectual, calm, and thoughtful than I expected." Liebig was at that time thought of as Professor of King's College, but the fact that he was not a member of the Church of England was fatal to the proposal.[1]

The researches on wax by the second Sir Benjamin Brodie were published in the "Philosophical Transactions of the Royal Society" in 1848. The same year he married Philothea Margaret, daughter of Serjeant Thompson. In 1849 he was elected a Fellow of the Royal Society, and in 1850 he received the Royal Medal for the above-mentioned researches. In 1855 he was appointed Waynflete Professor of Chemistry in the University of Oxford, and left London to reside there. In 1859–61 he was President

---

[1] See Appendix G. for some correspondence about Liebig's candidature at King's College.

of the Chemical Society, occupying that chair at the
same time that his father was presiding over the Royal
Society. A few years after this he suffered a very
severe illness, and in 1872 resigned the Chair of
Chemistry at Oxford to the regret of the whole
University. On leaving Oxford the Hon. Degree of
D.C.L. was conferred upon him at the Encænia, 1872.

He retired to his country house in Surrey, not
the one in which his father had lived, but situated
near it. He continued, however, to take a deep
interest in his own scientific work and in that of
others, and his last work, on "Ideal Chemistry,"
appeared only shortly before his death.

He died November 24, 1880, and was laid to rest
in Betchworth churchyard, which eighteen years
before had received the remains of his father, and
where little more than a year after, his wife was also
buried.

William, Brodie's younger son, was born in the
autumn of 1821. He was of a somewhat delicate
constitution in youth, and though sent at the age of
ten years to Harrow, he did not remain there very
long. After some private instruction he matriculated
at Trinity College, Cambridge, when seventeen years
old. He took his B.A. degree in 1843, and his M.A.
some two years later. In 1844 he was ordained
deacon, and was successively curate at Ewell and
Cheshunt. In 1851 he became rector of New
Alresford, and subsequently vicar of East Meon,
both in Hampshire.

He married Maria, daughter of William eighth

Earl Waldegrave, and sister of Viscount Chewton, who died from wounds received at the Alma, 1854. He died in the year 1882.

Maria, Brodie's only daughter, was married to the Rev. Edward Hoare, Hon. Canon of Canterbury. She died in 1863.

From this digression about Brodie's family I return to his own career in London after his marriage. He has himself left it on record in his Autobiography that at the time of his marriage his professional income had risen to £1,530, and that he had previously saved the money required to refurnish his house and prepare it for the reception of his bride. And as his income was rising rapidly, he need not have felt any anxiety beyond that dependence on health and the other incidents of life which is inseparable from all professional careers. Yet he speaks of this period as one of considerable anxiety, and a return of his dyspeptic symptoms still further troubled him. But he worked on bravely ; and in spite of the caution which was part of his character, and very probably derived from his Scotch ancestry, he thought himself justified in setting up his carriage and pair.

But he by no means ceased his scientific pursuits.[1] Though with his increasing practice, his hospital, and his lectures, his time was fully occupied, yet he found leisure to cultivate physiology ; and relates here some

[1] I remember a friend of Brodie telling me that some eminent French *savant*, on being told of his marriage, exclaimed, " Ah, poor fellow ! then all his scientific work is over." Brodie probably had heard this, and has therefore taken care to put on record the fact that immediately after his marriage he was busily at work at physiology.

experiments which he made at this time to illustrate the uses of the bile.

Brodie's rapidly increasing practice naturally brought him into connection with most of the prominent personages of the day, many of whom find a place, and a kindly notice, in his Autobiography; nor would any Life of Brodie be complete which did not include some notice of those whose friendship must have been so instrumental in building up the fabric of his fame and fortune.

The first person mentioned is Sir William Knighton, who had been originally a medical practitioner, and in that capacity accompanied the Marquis of Wellesley when he went to Spain on that diplomatic mission which had so important an influence on the country's history; for it was the support which Lord Wellington got from his brother's weight in the Ministry, and from the wise and courageous counsel which he would give his colleagues, that enabled him to carry on the war in the Peninsula in defiance of the malignant detraction of the favourers of Bonaparte in the press and in public, and in spite of the still more dangerous weakness and incapacity of those ministers whom Napier has held up to the deserved contempt of posterity. On his return from this employment Knighton soon abandoned his profession for a place at Court, which the favour of the Prince Regent offered to him — that of Keeper of the Privy Purse. Knighton's title to this favour was that he had become possessor of some papers, as executor to the late Sir John MacMahon, who had died as Keeper of the Privy Purse—papers which, Brodie says, "ought to have been destroyed"—and had taken these papers direct to the Regent, without disclosing their contents to any one. Ever since this piece of secret service Knighton had exercised great influence over the Regent, and when MacMahon's successor, Sir B. Bloomfield, was raised to the peerage and sent as ambassador to Stockholm, Knighton was appointed in his place. It was no doubt a coveted promotion ; but Brodie does not think that it tended to Sir William's happiness. He accepted the post against the advice of his wife, who seems to have been a person of far more elevation of character than her husband ; and her wisdom in that particular was speedily justified, for Sir William soon became as desirous of resigning as he had been of obtaining his post ; but his strong-minded wife convinced him that this would be dishonourable, since circumstances had not changed, and he still retained the King's confidence —who indeed left him his executor. But the significant fact is recorded by Brodie that he never had his wife, or son, or daughters presented at Court. No doubt the atmosphere of the Court at that time was very different from what it has since become.

He survived the King about six years, living in retirement at his house in Hampshire, and Brodie was one of only four friends who attended his funeral. His life had been a disappointment to himself, and the story, as told by Brodie, is a melancholy comment on the text, "Put not your trust in princes," though in this case at least the Prince seems to have in no way failed in his personal friendship for and confidence in his servant. Sir Benjamin speaks in warm terms of Knighton's character, his amiable manners, his knowledge of the world and practical sagacity, and plainly intimates that he was fitted for better things than to be a kind of upper servant, and that to a master whose service possibly involved complicity in actions of which he could not but disapprove.

Another of Brodie's intimate friends—indeed one nearly connected with his family—was Sir Richard Croft, the husband of one of Dr. Denman's daughters, whose connection with the Royal Family had a still more tragic end. He attended Princess Charlotte in her confinement in 1818, and was so overwhelmed by the popular outcry against his management of the case, that he committed suicide.

In 1819 Brodie moved into Savile Row, not into the house which he afterwards occupied No. 14, (where Sheridan was residing at the time of his death), but two doors from it, where now one of his successors at St. George's resides. This move, like all his other proceedings, seems not to have been taken till his means amply justified the expenditure, for he tells us that his professional income this year was £1,000 more than in the year preceding; and that from this time forward he laid by a considerable part of every year's earnings, so that he now began to build up the considerable fortune which he thought a necessary provision for his family. He was now only thirty-six years old; but his professional position was far higher than his age would seem to warrant; and though he was still only assistant surgeon at St. George's, he was rapidly rising to the largest practice in London. For Sir Astley Cooper, as he says, "had already begun to lose some of the vast reputation which he had previously enjoyed. Some one else was wanted, and I was ready to fill the vacant place."

No one indeed could fill it better, for Brodie had not only the activity and industry, the extensive pathological knowledge, and the keen insight of Cooper, but he had also the scholarly mind and the wide acquaintance with the world of science in which that great surgeon was deficient, and was as well qualified to hold his own with the leading spirits of the age, with the *savants* of the Royal Society, and the literary celebrities of Holland House, as with the magnates of the College of Surgeons.

In the same year, 1819, Lawrence having resigned his professorship of Comparative Anatomy and Physiology at the College of Surgeons, it was offered to and accepted by Brodie, who retained it for four years, and delivered four courses of lectures—two on the structure and functions of the organs of respiration and circulation, one on the organs of digestion, and the fourth on the nervous system. These lectures are not published *in extenso* in his collected works, though two of the most important are preserved, viz., the Introductory Lecture in 1820, and a most important and admirable one on the treatment of strangulation.[1]

[1] Vol. i. pp. 385, 407. Together with these should be read the tracts which follow, On the Mode of Death from Drowning, and on Light-

The strong, practical sense which raised Brodie to his position in the surgical world is nowhere more easily appreciated, even by those outside the profession, than in these minor works in which he treats of the accidents of everyday life.

These lectures were indeed to him a labour of love. We have seen how devoted he was to the study of physiology—and here he shows how stoically he sacrificed to his favourite study all the scanty hours of leisure that so busy a man might well have reserved for relaxation and the enjoyments of home. "Having," he says, "every year to make a fresh course of lectures on subjects on which I had not lectured previously was an almost frightful addition to my labours. It was only by giving up many hours which ought to have been devoted to sleep that I was able to fulfil my engagements, and even with this sacrifice," he characteristically adds, "I had not the satisfaction of knowing that my lectures were such as I could have wished them to be." We may be sure that Brodie was his own severest critic, and that his auditors recognised his mastery of the science, and the solid advances which he was making, while the lecturer was only regretting that he had not had the leisure to push them further. The composition of these lectures, he modestly adds, and the habit of recording his thoughts in writing, enabled him to

ning-stroke. But of the last, as too remote from ordinary experience to interest other than medical readers, I do not further speak. Nor do I think it necessary to do more than refer those of my readers who are interested in physiological matters to the Introductory Lecture for a clear, lively, and complete view of the state of science at that time.

detect his own deficiencies, and taught him to be less conceited of his own opinions than he should have been otherwise. The habit of taking written notes of the books he read was adopted at an early period of his life, though apparently in his more busy days he had to give it up, and he says that he still referred to these notes, at that late stage of his career, with satisfaction and with profit.

The two papers on the cognate subjects of the effects of strangulation and death from drowning were delivered as lectures at the College of Surgeons in 1821, but were not published till 1846. Why they were so long withheld from the public is not explained by their author; but they had been made use of in the treatise on Medical Jurisprudence of Dr. Paris and Mr. Fonblanque (1823), to whom Brodie communicated his notes on these subjects, or rather this subject, drowning being only a form of strangulation. The subject of these papers is of common interest; for the recovery of drowned persons is a matter of considerable public importance, especially in this country, where aquatic pursuits and pleasures are so common; and though other forms of strangulation are less commonly susceptible of treatment, still it is important that a medical man, who may be summoned in all haste to a suffocated person who cannot live more than a minute or two, unless he is properly treated, should know at once what to do. Now this is pointed out with unmistakable clearness in these lectures of Brodie; and they are also an admirable example of the sagacity with which he seized the essential points of a question, of the ingenuity with which he devised, and the accuracy with which he carried out, the experiments necessary to settle those points, and of the transparent clearness with which he explains them to his hearers, and deduces the practical conclusions to which they lead. The first essential point is to settle what is the cause of death in strangulation, and this is shown conclusively to be from the obstruction of the windpipe and the circulation through the nervous centres of non-oxygenated blood, causing first convulsions and then total suppression of the nervous functions, and consequent cessation of the heart's action.[1] It is also shown that there is a brief interval during which the action of the heart can be restored by artificial respiration; but that after that interval nothing can restore it. Hence the importance is shown of instant resort to artificial respiration. And it is also proved that the circulation of dark or venous blood through the brain acts as a narcotic poison on that organ, so that, even after the heart's action has been restored by the introduction of air into the lungs, danger is not over; and, on the recurrence of symptoms, treatment must be as prompt and as well directed as at first.

All this is, of course, familiar enough now. But it was not so three-quarters of a century ago. Then all sorts of useless and even mischievous things were

---

[1] We must recollect that this first and vital point was then far from being ascertained. So eminent a surgeon as Larrey taught (as Paris and Fonblanque tell us) that death from drowning is caused by the entrance of water into the lungs.

done to drowned persons ; and time was lost in cases where the delay of a few seconds may make the difference between life and death.

And let us not forget that an additional merit of the treatment which Brodie showed to be the essential condition for the recovery of the drowned is its simplicity. We are familiar now with " First aid to the wounded," and ambulance classes, by which non-professional, and even uneducated persons, such as policemen, dock-labourers, and others have been taught how to resuscitate the drowned. And such persons are much more likely than a medical man to see the patient while resuscitation is possible. Thus lives have been preserved which there is much reason to think would have been sacrificed if time had been spent in seeking for medical aid. The methods of artificial respiration have been improved since Brodie's day ; but the physiological reasoning on which he based the treatment of this too common accident neither has been improved nor indeed can be.

It is of course true that in thus teaching that artificial respiration is the essential point in the treatment of the drowned, Brodie was only following what John Hunter had said more than thirty years previously.[1] But Brodie had studied the subject much more profoundly and more systematically than his great predecessor ; he had devised a much more connected and convincing series of experiments, and was thus enabled

---

[1] Proposals for the Recovery of Persons Apparently Drowned, " Phil. Trans.," vol. lxvi. (Mar. 21, 1776) ; Hunter's Works by Palmer, iv. 165.

to avoid the chief error into which Hunter fell, in denying the deleterious effects of the circulation of impure blood through the brain.

It was in the year 1821, while he was still lecturing at the College of Surgeons, that he was first consulted by the King. The matter was one of no further importance than as bringing him into personal relations with George IV., for it was only a question of removing a small sebaceous tumour from the scalp, and even this simple operation was not performed by him, but by Sir Astley Cooper, in the presence of a formidable array of eminent surgeons and physicians. But it is curious to read that, to salve the mortification of Sir Everard Home (who had been originally consulted in the matter) at being thus superseded by Cooper, "his son, who was then a very young lieutenant in the navy, was advanced rather prematurely to the rank of commander." Such were the vagaries of patronage in the days of our fathers. From this time forward, however, though Brodie had no official position at Court, he was constantly consulted by the King along with Sir Astley Cooper, and when the latter was gazetted in 1828 to the office of Sergeant-Surgeon, Brodie succeeded him as Surgeon in Ordinary to his Majesty.

It was not long after this time, viz., in July, 1822, that on the resignation of Mr. Griffiths, on account of ill health, Brodie became surgeon to St. George's Hospital, after acting as assistant-surgeon for fourteen years. As we have seen, however, his peculiar position there gave him really as much hospital practice as if he had been nominally surgeon, perhaps even more, for during the Peninsular War he was in charge of half of Mr. Gunning's patients, as well as having the chief share in the treatment of those of Sir Everard Home. Gunning returned to England, and resumed his hospital duties after the battle of Waterloo.

On Brodie's appointment as surgeon, Home persuaded the Governors to appoint one of Brodie's juniors, Mr. Ewbank, as his assistant, to see after his patients. Ewbank became surgeon in 1823, on Gunning's resignation, and then Jeffreys was appointed as Home's assistant. He again became surgeon on Ewbank's death in 1825, and Rose was then made Home's assistant, a proposal to appoint him assistant surgeon to the hospital having been made and negatived. Home himself kept the title and appointment of surgeon from 1793 to 1827, but for the last nineteen years of his tenure of office, though he gave a course of twelve lectures every year, he seems not to have had any real duties to perform towards the patients. Truly we manage some things, at any rate, better in these days!

The following year was made memorable to Brodie by the death of Sir Thomas Plumer, the Master of the Rolls, whose friendship and patronage had done so much for him while he was still young and struggling for success; and still more so by that of Dr. Matthew Baillie. This eminent man was a native of Scotland, and was born in the year 1757; he was the nephew of the Hunters, John and William, and had borne the chief part in the anatomical teaching in Dr. William Hunter's school. At the age of thirty he married the elder daughter of Dr. Denman, who had married Brodie's aunt. Dr. Baillie was one of the physicians to St. George's Hospital at the time of the sudden death of his uncle, John Hunter, in that hospital ; and his mild temper and kindly manners had, as it seems, done what was possible to smooth the quarrels which Hunter's violence and roughness had done so much to aggravate. He was present when that great man breathed his last. Baillie was, I believe, the first English author who wrote exclusively on morbid anatomy—a science which he had studied under those supreme masters by whom he was educated.[1] He was equally successful in practical medicine, and is said by Brodie to have acquired a larger practice than that of any other physician since the days of Radcliffe and Mead. The labour of conducting so great a practice was immense. He rose at six o'clock, was busily at work with correspondents and patients till a late dinner, and even then had to make another round of visits, and was seldom in bed before midnight. The incessant labour told both on his spirits and his health, and Brodie says that he would doubtless have been a more happy man, and lived longer, had he been professionally less successful. He retired from the hospital very early, before he was forty years of age ; and his increasing practice obliged him for some years before he died to limit himself strictly to consultations, and to his attendance at Windsor on George III. during

[1] It is Baillie's face which is shown on the medallion of the Pathological Society, surrounded by the striking epigraph, "Nec silet mors."

his years of seclusion. He died worn out at the age of sixty-two, while his son, who pursued a more even and tranquil course, lived in health and vigour to the age of ninety-seven, and his sister Agnes to over a hundred. His sister Joanna was long the only English poetess who had obtained a place on the roll of fame, and her dramatic and poetical works, though little read now, were enthusiastically praised by Sir Walter Scott, and are still highly esteemed by good judges. She also, as well as her sister Agnes, lived to extreme old age. One of the most graceful memories of Dr. Baillie is that of his resigning to John Hunter the family estate in Scotland which William Hunter had left to him, doubtless on account of his quarrel with his brother John. Baillie, recognising that it ought to belong to John Hunter, refused to avail himself of the legacy. Baillie was one of the many great men who have served St. George's Hospital, and his portrait there speaks to that kindly, liberal disposition which all tradition ascribes to him. The slight and somewhat mournful notice of him in Brodie's Autobiography comes as an appropriate pendant to that of Sir W. Knighton, not that these "consolations to the obscure" are ever far to seek. But, as Knighton's history is a good example of the disappointment which often follows success in pushing oneself by the ways of ordinary ambition and Court favour, so Baillie's equally shows the folly of sacrificing life and health, good spirits and good temper in order to slave at the professional mill. Many men do this merely from love of money ; but all that we know of Baillie shows that

G

this was not his weakness. A few, and very few, like his great predecessor, John Hunter, are driven to work at science, as St. Paul was driven to preach the gospel, by a necessity laid upon them, which they cannot resist, even if they would. But in Baillie's case it seems as if he sacrificed his life and his comfort to that nearly irresistible "fetish" of custom, which rides so many of us like the Old Man of the Sea, and drives us round a daily track which has long become dull and tasteless, but which we have no energy to quit.

Another, and a far greater, name meets us in the record which Brodie has left of this period of his life—that of Dr. Thomas Young. He also may be said to have sacrificed his life to his zeal for labour, for he died in 1829 at the age of fifty-five, worn out, it would seem, by labours too gigantic for any soul still inhabiting its tenement of clay.[1] He, indeed, of all moderns, most nearly approached to the daring of the old philosophers who aspired to know everything which is the subject of knowledge. "His was one of the most profound minds," says Helmholtz, " that the world has ever seen. . . . He excited the wonder of his contemporaries, who, however, were unable to follow him to the heights at which his daring intellect was accustomed to soar. His most important ideas lay, therefore, buried and for-

---

[1] " A fiery soul which, working out its way,
Fretted the pigmy body to decay,
And o'er-informed its tenement of clay."

DRYDEN.

gotten in the folios of the Royal Society, until a new generation gradually and painfully made the same discoveries, and proved the exactness of his assertions and the truth of his demonstrations." This passage is quoted by Tyndall in his treatise on "Light," in which he does not hesitate to class Young as the greatest philosopher since Newton's day, and in intellectual stature not very much inferior to Newton, and he illustrates the book by a copy of the portrait of Young which adorns the Board-room of St. George's Hospital.

Tyndall's tribute to Young is, of course, in recognition of the fact that he was the founder of the undulatory theory of light. But Young was equally great in other departments of learning. Languages, ancient and modern, were housed within his brain, and, to use the words of his epitaph, "he first penetrated the obscurity which had veiled for ages the hieroglyphics of Egypt."[1] But it was no doubt true, as Helmholtz adds, that "he had the misfortune to be too much in advance of his age," and the fact is witnessed by Brodie's somewhat contemptuous notice of him—not that he says anything personally disrespectful of Young—in fact, he calls him "one of the greatest philosophers of his age"—but he puts him on a lower rank than Davy as a philosopher—an estimate which would have surprised Tyndall—and he rates him low indeed as a physician, placing him much below Dr. Chambers and Dr. Nevinson. This is the only instance in which there seems reason to

[1] Tyndall on Light, 2nd ed., 1875, p. 50.

doubt the perfect accuracy (perhaps the perfect im-
partiality) of Brodie's judgment. No doubt Dr.
Young had no great success as a physician; but
there is no reason for thinking that he ever sought
it, and it is quite possible to account for this fact
otherwise than by adopting the explanation which
Dr. Peacock gives of it in his Life of Young,
viz., that he was above certain ignoble arts of
which his competitors made use. It seems obvious
that Dr. Young was too much occupied with his
various and profound studies to give that exclusive
devotion to the practice of medicine which is necessary for conspicuous success. But when Brodie goes
on to say that he "could never discern that Young
kept any written notes of cases," and that he
doubted "whether he ever thought of his cases
in the hospital after he left the wards," he shows
evidently that he is speaking with imperfect information, and in all probability with some bias. By
a fortunate accident, when Dr. J. A. Wilson was
appointed physician to St. George's on Young's
death, in the year 1829, a volume of notes of
hospital cases for the years 1828–29 under the care
of Dr. Young was passed on to him, and was by
him handed over to his son-in-law and successor at
the hospital, Dr. Howship Dickinson, who has given
an interesting *resumé* of it in the *St. George's Hospital
Gazette* for May 10, 1893. These notes comprise
145 cases, and are "ample and minute in treatment," though less specific in clinical and pathological details. I cannot do better than quote Dr.

Dickinson's account of the effect which the perusal of these notes produced on Dr. Wilson — a man of all others least disposed to take too enthusiastic a view of his contemporaries or predecessors. Dr. Wilson writes thus in 1845 : "For many years past, by a system of mock-energy in the treatment of disease, reckless in its means, because opposed to reflection, and pretending to facts from the absence of principles, the study of physic has been discouraged in this country, and its practice degraded ;" and subsequently, looking back upon the practice of Dr. Young, and his want of popularity as a physician, his successor thus explains the position of the elder philosopher : "He lived in an age when what is called *vigorous practice* was very generally prevalent ; when the use of calomel and the lancet was in the ascendant ; when symptoms were rudely interfered with and combated without any proper study of the causes in which they originated." Dr. Dickinson thus sums up the case : "Dr. Young had the caution of a philosopher, Dr. Wilson the temper of a sceptic. The public asked neither for philosophy nor scepticism, but, like Christian and Hopeful, preferred to follow Mr. Vain Confidence, too often, like them, to find themselves in the clutches of Giant Despair." I cannot, in a work not intended exclusively for professional readers, go further into the details of Dr. Young's practice as here recorded by Dr. Dickinson, interesting as they are to medical men. They seem to me to account very fairly for the fact, vouched for by the apothecary to the hospital of that day, that the proportion of cures in Dr. Young's patients was greater than in those of his colleagues, by the simple explanation that his practice was less meddle-some—that he was less under the dominion of the " antiphlogistic " superstition than his less philo-sophic colleagues—in fact, interfered less with what he must have felt that he did not fully understand. Brodie's explanation of the fact (which he does not contest) is that his colleagues, having higher reputa-tions as practical physicians, had graver cases sent to them ; but this, though no doubt possible, is sup-ported by no evidence, and for my own part I prefer to think that the great philosopher was also a scientific and competent physician, and to some extent anticipated the more common-sense practice of the present day, though he does not seem to have bent his mighty genius seriously to medical problems,[1] nor to have cared to waste his life as Baillie did in making money which he did not value and could not spend.

[1] There was an old story at St. George's of some altercation between Young and his colleagues, in which he said, "I could take a half-sheet of note-paper and write down on it your whole art and science of medicine"—no difficult task when bleeding, mercury, and purging comprised by far the greatest part of it.

V

1823–1834

Full Tide of Success

Brodie in his busiest time—More of Brodie's contemporaries—Jeffreys, Rose, Sir E. Home, and the destruction of John Hunter's MSS.— Brodie in personal attendance on the King—Death of George IV. —Appointed Serjeant-Surgeon—Formation of a complete School of Medicine at Kinnerton Street—Election of Mr. Cutler at St. George's Hospital, and consequent disagreement between Brodie and some of his colleagues—System of hospital elections.

> Seggendo in piuma,
> In fama non si vien, nè sotto coltre ;
> Senza la qual chi sua vita consuma,
>   Cotal vestigio in terra di sè lascia,
> Qual fumo in aere, od in acqua la schiuma.
> DANTE.

BRODIE was now in the full tide of success. He relates that his professional income, which amounted in 1816, the year of his marriage, to £1,530 had risen in 1823 to £6,500, and while the smaller sum included an amount (not stated) derived from lectures, such receipts are excluded from the larger sum, which represents only the proceeds of private practice. And this large income went on steadily

increasing from year to year. No one practised more
sedulously than Brodie that "assiduous waiting" on
fortune which Burns prescribes to his youthful friend.[1]
He never, in the height of his prosperity, he tells us,
"absented himself from London for more than three
weeks in the summer, and sometimes not at all,"
though he got a little country air by living at Hampstead in the empty season, and coming to London
after an early breakfast. This devotion to business
earned its reward. As Sir Astley Cooper's practice
declined, Brodie more and more took his place as the
leading London surgeon, and he notices that his
practice as an operator specially increased, though, as
he himself remarks, he had no particular liking for
this part of his duties, and I have been told (for I
never myself had an opportunity of seeing him
operate) was not specially remarkable for manual
dexterity in his operations. He seems however to
have been successful with his cases — nor is this
wonderful, for success in operative surgery depends
more on care in the after-treatment than on manual
dexterity (at least, in the ordinary run of operations),
and Brodie excelled most men in care and in
sagacity in interpreting symptoms and catching the
indications for treatment.[2] Of only one operation
does Brodie say that it gave him any real concern

---

[1] See motto to Chapter III.
[2] I may give here an illustration for my medical readers. Brodie had
had occasion to tie the external iliac artery at the hospital, and had been
obliged to leave town on a professional call soon afterwards. His
assistant found the patient feverish, and with much discomfort about the
wound. Ascribing this to peritonitis he put the man on a course of

—that of lithotomy ; and it was this concern, no doubt, which rendered him peculiarly apt to receive and adopt the suggestion which originated at Paris with Civiale to crush the stone instead of extracting it through a wound. Brodie's services in promoting this important improvement in practical surgery are spoken of on page 153.

Considerable changes had taken place in the staff of St. George's Hospital at the period with which we are now dealing. Mr. Gunning and Sir Everard Home had resigned. Mr. Keate thus became Senior Surgeon, and remained so, long after Brodie's retirement. Mr. Ewbank, who succeeded to Mr. Gunning's vacancy in 1823, only held the appointment till 1825, when he died and was replaced by Jeffreys, who was Brodie's senior at the hospital, and had, as we have seen, taught him the art of note-taking, in which he afterwards so far surpassed his teacher,[1] and in 1827, when Sir Everard Home resigned, Mr. Rose was elected, whose early death in 1829 deprived the profession of one who had already done some very good work, and who would have done much more if his life had been prolonged. He, like Jeffreys, had served in the army, and a paper of his, in the "Medico-Chirurgical

mercury and the usual "antiphlogistic" regimen. Before this could have done much harm Brodie returned to town, and at once drove to see his patient. Recognising that the symptom depended not on peritonitis, but on pent-up suppuration, he broke open the wound, put the patient on a more generous regimen, and saved his life. Had the assistant performed the operation, even if he had done it more neatly and speedily, the result would probably have been different.

[1] Jeffreys had been away from England, serving with the army in Spain.

Transactions," based on his military experience, is still referred to as being the commencement of the healthy reaction against the abuse of mercury—an abuse that had attained such an appalling height, and was so vigorously denounced by Sir Astley Cooper. Of Rose Brodie says : "My intimacy with him tended very much to the improvement of my own character, and I look back to the friendship which existed between us as one of the most happy circumstances of my life." Mr. Rose belonged to a family which had a tendency to pulmonary disease, and in the year 1828 he had the misfortune to lose three out of his four children from scarlet fever. The calamity " broke his heart. The disease of which his brothers and sisters had been the victims became developed in himself and he soon followed his children to the grave."

Perhaps this may be as convenient a place as any other for dealing with a topic which the biographer of Brodie cannot escape, though it is not one on which any attached son of St. George's cares to dwell. I mean the character of Sir Everard Home. He had now, as we have seen, retired from the service of the hospital, and he only survived his retirement two years, during which time he bore the courtesy title of Consulting Surgeon, a compliment which was not paid to either Brodie or Keate. Home was, I think we may take it, a man of considerable talent and distinction. Brodie was evidently much attached to him, and does all that he honestly can to soften the condemnation which, for all that, he cannot altogether avoid. I see no reason for not accepting the estimate of his professional character which Brodie gave of him in the Hunterian Oration of 1837, and which he deliberately re-quotes in the Autobiography. " He was a great practical surgeon. His mind went direct to the leading points of the case before him, disregarding all those minor points by which minds of smaller capacity are perplexed and misled. Hence his views of disease were clear, and were such as were easily communicated to his pupils, and his practice was simple and decided. He never shrank from difficulties ; but, on the contrary, seemed to have pleasure in meeting and overcoming them ; and I am satisfied that to this one of his qualities many of his patients were indebted for their lives." He was successful in practice, though he never obtained the reputation or the income of Astley Cooper or Brodie, and if he had confined himself to surgery only, he would have left a name which perhaps now might not be much remembered outside of St. George's Hospital, but would there be respected and reckoned on about the same level as that of Sir Cæsar Hawkins, or any other of the numerous Serjeant Surgeons who grace the rolls of its surgical staff.

Unluckily for his good name, he was intimately connected with the greatest medical philosopher of the age—John Hunter—who had married his sister, and whom he assisted in his researches in a subordinate capacity, until, as it seems, he began to think himself equal to the task of undertaking his master's suc-cession, and filling the place left vacant by his sudden death. To this he was wholly inadequate. I have

not myself read any of his scientific works, but I
believe they are of little value, and there can be no
doubt that what value they have is chiefly derived
from their including original matter taken from
Hunter's notes, which of course came into Home's
possession as one of Hunter's executors, and the one,
as it would seem, who took the leading part in
obtaining the sanction of Parliament to the purchase
of the Hunterian Museum, of which Hunter's MSS.
were an integral part, and of which they would at
this day have been a most precious portion, had they
been preserved. But this unfortunately is not the
case. Home destroyed them with his own hand, and
the fact must always remain as an indelible blot on his
memory. The defence which Sir Everard himself
made for his conduct (for he neither did nor could
deny that he had, with his own hand, burned the
papers) made the matter rather worse than better for
him. He said, first, that he had a legal right to the
papers, which were no part of the Museum. In the
Museum he could have no interest except that of a
trustee, bound to preserve every part of it, and deliver
it entire to the purchasers. But no intelligent person
could for a moment doubt that the MSS. descriptive
of the preparations were an integral part of them; and
as a matter of fact the Museum would have lost much
of its value, had not Clift previously taken copies
of many of Hunter's notes on the preparations, the
originals of which were among the papers that Home
destroyed. This fact alone convicts Home of a breach
of trust, and his pettifogging plea, that the MSS. were

not specifically included in the will, makes the case against him only the stronger. His second assertion, that Hunter had himself told him to destroy them is justly stigmatised by Mr. Drewry Ottley [1] as "incredible"; and he further calls attention to the fact that Home kept these papers during the years which elapsed before the purchase of the Museum, and only burned them when they would otherwise have been handed over to the purchasers. No one, in fact, doubts that the reason why he burned Hunter's notes was to avoid the detection that would otherwise have been inevitable of the extent to which he had dressed himself out in Hunter's plumes. "Home contributed," says Mr. Ottley, "more papers to the Royal Society than any other single member of that distinguished body since its foundation." If these papers were indeed largely pillaged from Hunter's MSS., he had great temptation to make away with those MSS.; while, if they were not, the preservation of the papers would have been most desirable in Home's own interest, as it would have vindicated their originality.

Sir Benjamin Brodie is a witness as favourably disposed to the accused as could possibly be found; but his regard for truth compels him practically to give the case up. He says he had frequent opportunities of seeing these papers during the nine or ten years in which he, along with Clift, assisted Home in his dissections; that they consisted of rough notes, not useful to any one except Hunter, though he thinks they

---

[1] "Life of Hunter." Palmer's Edition of Hunter's Works. Vol. i. p. 152.

might have assisted Owen in completing the catalogue
(a fact which made it therefore Home's duty to
preserve them)—that "in pursuing his own investigations Home sometimes referred to them; but I
must say that while I was connected with him I
never knew an instance in which he did not scrupu-
lously acknowledge whatever he took from them.
Unhappily he was led afterwards to deviate from this
right course, and in his later publications I recognise
some things which he has given us as the result of his
own observation, though they were really taken from
Hunter's notes and drawings." Nothing further
need, I think, be said on this unpleasant subject.[1]

Home seems in the last years of his life to have
become a man of pleasure and fashion, a *bon vivant*,
and a boon companion of the Prince Regent, and so
to have neglected both professional and scientific
pursuits, as he seems to have become careless of the
dictates of gratitude, friendship, and honour.

In the year 1830 Brodie's attendance on the King,
which had previously, as we have seen, been inter-
mittent, became constant and personal. George IV.
was dying of dropsy from heart-disease, and he derived
much benefit from Brodie's attendance, and conceived
a warm personal attachment for his kind and skilful
surgeon, so that Brodie had to go every night to
Windsor after an early dinner, sleep there, and return
to London in the morning. His habit was to go into

[1] A full account of this matter and the report of Mr. Clift's evidence
about it before a Parliamentary Committee will be found in Mr. S.
Paget's "Life of John Hunter," pp. 250, *et seq.*

the King's room at about six o'clock, and sit talking with him for an hour or two before leaving for town. He seems to have formed a more indulgent estimate of the King's character than those now in vogue, and which are based, to a great extent, on the somewhat slapdash criticism of Thackeray's "Four Georges." "He would have been," he says, "a happier and a better man if it had been his lot to be nothing more than a simple country gentleman, instead of being in the exalted situation which he inherited. If William IV. retained his simplicity of character, and his freedom from selfishness, it was because he ascended the throne at a late period of life, having had no previous expectation that he would ever be thus elevated."

The following account of the death of George IV. has not, I believe, been published. It is contained in a communication to Sir Benjamin Brodie from Sir Wathen Waller which was preserved amongst his correspondence :—

> "POPE'S VILLA,
> "5 o'clock, evening,
> "Aug. 11, 1830.

"I am this moment, my dear Sir, favoured with your note, and its Enclosure. . . . You desired a copy of the hasty account I gave his Majesty of the few last moments of my *beloved* and Royal Master. I now enclose it with an assurance of the *high* Regard I shall ever feel for *you* from the very judicious, honorable, and manly Conduct you evinced during your Attendance on the late King, which will ever remain *strongly* impressed on the Recollection of

" Your most sincerely,

" J. W. WALLER.

" At half-past eleven o'clock on Friday night, June 25th, his late Majesty, not finding himself worse than he had been for some time past, dismissed Sir Henry Halford, who had been in attendance since seven o'clock in the morning, and sent him to bed.

" His Majesty then composed himself for the night, the pages retired to the outer room, and the King soon fell asleep, in the same position to which he had lately been accustomed, leaning on a table prepared for that express purpose and placed before him, with his forehead on one hand, and the hand of Sir Wathen Waller, who was sitting up with him, in the other. His Majesty slept quietly till a quarter before two, Saturday morning, when he awoke and asked for his medicine. This he took, and drank after it a little clove tea. The King then resumed his former posture and again slept quietly till a quarter before three. His Majesty was all the time in an armchair (for he had not been in a bed for many weeks) and ordered the windows to be thrown open, as had been his custom for some time past during both night and day. The King then expressed himself a little faint and desired some sal-volatile and water. This he endeavoured several times to swallow, but could not. Sir Henry Halford was immediately called. His Majesty then pressed the hand of Sir Wathen Waller which still remained in his more strongly, and looking him full in the face exclaimed distinctly, 'My boy! this is Death,' and immediately closed his eyes and reclined back in his chair. At this instant Sir Henry Halford entered the room and took his Majesty's hand, but the King never spoke afterwards, and with a very few short breathings expired exactly as the clock struck a quarter-past three on Saturday morning, June 26, 1830. Before this, however, Sir William Knighton, Sir Mathew Tierney, and Mr. Brodie, who had also been summoned, but whose appartments were more distant from the chamber of his Majesty than those of Sir Henry Halford, entered the room, and were also present during the last moments of his Majesty's life."

It was early in King William's reign that Brodie succeeded Sir Everard Home as Serjeant-Surgeon, an office secured to the holder for his life, and which therefore Brodie continued to hold in the present reign till his death. Brodie's pupil and successor at St. George's Hospital, Sir Prescott Hewett, was the last person to be appointed to this post. On Hewett's death his vacancy was not filled up, Sir James Paget being now the sole Serjeant-Surgeon, and it seems probable that the office will cease to exist. It is, in fact, only nominal, for it does not carry with it any real duties. Brodie, for instance, though Serjeant-Surgeon during nearly the whole of William IV.'s reign, never attended that king personally. Still the Serjeant-Surgeoncy has always been regarded as one of the few honours accessible to the medical pro-

fession, and a mark of recognition of the two acknowledged leaders of the surgical world of London ; and
its extinction will be witnessed with regret, though
we cannot but allow that the office has ceased to be
necessary now that the sovereign's personal presence
with the army has become almost an impossibility, the
especial duty of the Serjeant-Surgeon having been to
attend the King whenever he joined his troops.[1]

When Brodie declined to take over the anatomical
museum of Mr. Wilson and purchase the goodwill of
his school in Windmill Street, he built a theatre of
his own in another house in that street for surgical
lectures, and founded a museum of preparations illustrative of surgical pathology, which now forms the
nucleus of the museum of St. George's Hospital.
The fees of the students who entered to these surgical
courses formed a part of his professional income, and
are entered in Sir Benjamin's fee-books with the
scrupulous accuracy and business-like regularity which
marked all his proceedings. But they formed so
small a part of the large total of his professional
income, and the labour was so serious an addition to
his already too numerous engagements, that it is
evident that he continued to lecture more for the
love of the employment than for the profit it brought
him. In those days, as we have said above, lectures
were given in the evening, and Brodie says : "I had
often scarcely time to eat a hasty dinner before I
proceeded to the lecture-room, and then, almost
immediately after my lecture was concluded, had to

[1] See Appendix H for correspondence about Brodie's appointment.

visit patients who required a second visit during the
twenty-four hours, or whom I had been prevented
from visiting in the early part of the day." And
after he got home there was his heavy correspondence
to deal with before he went to bed, " besides having
not unfrequently to make journeys into the country
which occupied a considerable portion of the night."
In spite of the large amount of work which he had on
hand, however, he was accustomed to write regularly
every week to his son at school. Many of these
letters were written, as he says in them, " in the
carriage jolting over the stones of London," or on
long drives to visit patients. No wonder that he
began to feel the necessity of giving up his lectures.
But this he could not manage till 1830, when he
transferred his class at Windmill Street to his junior
colleagues. These were Mr. Cæsar Hawkins, Sir Cæsar
Hawkins's grandson (and Serjeant-Surgeon afterwards,
as his grandfather and great-uncle had been), who
was appointed Surgeon to the Hospital in 1829 on
Mr. Rose's death, and Mr. Babington, who was
Assistant-Surgeon in 1829 and Surgeon in 1830, when
Mr. Jeffreys retired. But Brodie continued to impart
surgical instruction (which indeed he seems to have
regarded as his duty), from the full store of his
experience, to the pupils of the hospital in the form
of clinical lectures, delivered in the early part of the
day, in the lecture theatre of the hospital. And now
the formation of the Hospital Medical School began.
It was in the year 1831, according to Dr. Page,[1] that

[1] " St. George's Hospital Reports," vol. i. p. 11.

a complete school of medicine and surgery was first established in the walls of the hospital, though the students had still to go elsewhere for anatomical instruction. Dr. Page names Sir Benjamin Brodie and Mr. Cæsar Hawkins as joint lecturers on surgery. The students went for their anatomical instruction, some to the old school in Windmill Street, where Mr. Herbert Mayo and Mr. Cæsar Hawkins lectured on anatomy and physiology; some to a school founded by Mr. S. Lane in his own house, close to the hospital,[1] where he and Dr. Wilson lectured. From this division of the two schools sprang a long quarrel, which disturbed Brodie's later days, and which must be noticed in any complete account of his life, though, as all the actors in it have long passed away, and the papers bearing on it have been mostly destroyed, no very confident history of it can now be given; nor perhaps is it necessary. Still some judgment must be formed about it by any one who wishes to pronounce a mature opinion on Brodie's character.

It is this conviction which leads me to discuss a topic that otherwise I would have avoided, since I cannot honestly acquit the subject of my biography of all blame, in my own opinion, in the matter. But I must again repeat that at this period it can but be a matter of opinion. No judicial conclusion is possible now that the actors have all passed away, and much of the evidence on both sides has perished. It was a transaction with regard to which Brodie's conduct

---

[1] This house stood in or close to Tattersall's Yard on a site now occupied by part of Grosvenor Crescent.

was severely and publicly censured by his enemies,
and the strongest aspersions were freely cast on his
motives. These aspersions I most sincerely disbelieve.
I think he acted from pure and honest motives, even
when I hold that he erred in judgment ; and I may
plead that, though I was too young to recollect the
things themselves, I was well acquainted with most of
the actors in them. In particular I was privileged to
enjoy the friendship both of Mr. Cutler, on the one
side, and Dr. Wilson on the other, from the time that
I studied surgery and medicine under them as masters
down to the end of their long lives. I may therefore,
at least claim to be impartial in the question.

In the *Lancet*, February 10, 1883, is an admirable
biographical notice of Dr. Wilson by his son-in-law,
Dr. Howship Dickinson. Here an account is given
of this unfortunate disagreement, the accuracy of
which cannot be questioned on the side of Brodie's
opponents ; for Dr. Dickinson was so kind as to let
me see a letter which Mr. Samuel Lane wrote to him
after reading the paper, in which Mr. Lane completely
sanctions his narrative. .I may quote from this narrative the following succinct account of the matter: "In
1829, upon the death of Dr. Thos. Young, Dr. Wilson
was elected Physician to St. George's Hospital. Up
to this time his career had been one of great success
and great promise ; honours had been nobly achieved,
difficulties manfully overcome ; he possessed social
influence, professional support, and hospital position.
But, far from leading smoothly on to fortune, his
appointment at St. George's appears to have led

mainly to trouble and disputes. Whatever may have been the rights of these, it is clear that with his accession the staff of St. George's acquired the elements of discord. When Dr. Wilson became Physician to the Hospital, Mr. Brodie had been Surgeon for seven years; he had acquired great influence both with the public and at the hospital, and was accustomed to the possession and exercise of power. Dr. Wilson had been used to the exalted respect of a somewhat small circle; he did not readily acknowledge a superior in any one; he was eloquent, combative, and intrepid. Mr. Brodie had the support of his colleagues and the board. Dr. Wilson had a mean opinion of both bodies, and no cordial relations with either. It is easy to foresee what must necessarily have followed. The disagreement culminated, after the manner of hospitals, at a contested election."

I conclude from this and from other things I have heard both from Dr. Dickinson and other friends of Dr. Wilson, and from what I knew of the latter myself (and I knew him well, and respected him highly), that Dr. Wilson was irritated by the obvious superiority of Brodie's position at the hospital, and that he did not make due allowance for the fact that Brodie (who was twelve years his senior, and had been one of his teachers) had fairly earned his pre-eminence by hard work and good service to the hospital. "Dr. Wilson," says his biographer, "thought highly of himself, and with reason. He was apt to form too low an estimate of his fellow-men." And very probably he did not recognise, and would not have admitted, the fact that Brodie, though doubtless inferior to himself as a scholar, and possibly as a speaker, and less accomplished in many ways, was yet far his superior in practical ability. And to these causes of discord were added private matters arising out of the intimate connection which had subsisted between Brodie and the elder Wilson,[1] and between Dr. James Arthur Wilson and Mr. Lane, who had been a house-pupil of Dr. Wilson's father, Mr. James Wilson. Everything therefore was prepared for the definite breach which followed on the occurrence of a vacancy in the surgical staff of the hospital in 1834.

The position of the Windmill Street school was inconvenient for students attending at St. George's; and in those days, when there was but one examination at the College of Surgeons, and that at the end of the curriculum, in anatomy and physiology as well as surgery, the student continued his studies in the dissecting-room till the end of his hospital career. The natural course would have been to adopt Mr. Lane's anatomical school as a part of the hospital school; but this obvious arrangement was prevented

---

[1] Brodie never concealed the obligations which he was under to Mr. Wilson, whom he admired for his eminent qualities as an anatomical teacher, and to whom he owed his first introduction into the ranks of public teachers of medicine, through the appointment which Wilson gave him in the Windmill Street school. As there was so much dissension afterwards between him and Mr. Wilson's son, it is well to put on record that to the father Brodie owed very much of his advancement in life, though, of course, he owed far more to the talent and energy with which he used the opportunities that Mr. Wilson's school offered him.

by some personal disagreement between Mr. Lane with Dr. Wilson on one side, and Brodie with his friends on the other. The cause of quarrel remains now a matter of conjecture, but it seems probable that Mr. Lane would not join the hospital school unless assured of Brodie's powerful support at the next vacancy in the surgical staff of the hospital, while Brodie was determined to procure, if possible, the election of Mr. Cutler, who was then assisting him in his private practice. And as a matter of fact, Mr. Cutler was elected in 1834,[1] to the great indignation of Mr. Lane and his friends—an indignation for which there was some justification. Mr. Cutler was an honoured and dear friend of my own, and a most excellent practical surgeon,[2] one of whom I would be the last to speak otherwise than in the terms of praise which he fully deserved ; but no one could say that, at that time at all events, his reputation

---

[1] The election took place on November 7th, on which day also the celebrated Dr. Hope was elected Assistant Physician. The interest which the struggle excited is shown by the large number (301) who attended and voted. Mr. Cutler obtained an absolute majority over his two competitors, Mr. Lane and Mr. Palmer, the editor of John Hunter's works. The numbers were : Cutler, 179 ; Lane, 99 ; Palmer, 23.

[2] It was said of Mr. Cutler, who had a considerable practice both in lithotomy and lithotrity, in private as well as in hospital, that he never lost a patient after either operation. Whether this was literally true I cannot say ; but he was certainly most successful in these and all other operations on the genito-urinary organs. Nor was his success confined to that special branch of surgery. But he never took, and I believe refused to take, any part in the public teaching of the students, though his pithy remarks as he went round the wards were most useful, and live still in the memory of his pupils.

as an anatomist and possibly as a surgeon[1] could
compare with Lane's ; and it has, I think, been the
almost unanimous opinion of those who knew all
the facts, that in this instance Brodie allowed his
feelings of friendship to blind him to the true interests
of the hospital. Dr. Wilson naturally sided with his
fellow-lecturer and his father's house-pupil, Mr. Lane.
And in Dr. Wilson's case there were no doubt private
reasons for disagreement, arising out of the long
connection between Brodie and Dr. Wilson's father,
the celebrated anatomist. This connection involved
some pecuniary obligation, and it is believed that this
obligation was felt as galling by Wilson and his family,
though from what I have heard I do not think that
Brodie was otherwise than most generous in his
behaviour in the matter. At any rate, there was,
as Dr. Dickinson's biography plainly shows, some
private cause which made Dr. Wilson quick enough
to take up his colleague's quarrel, and as he was a
man of great talents and a forcible speaker the
contention waxed hot between them. In the year
1836 the school, which claimed to be specially that
of St. George's Hospital, was opened at Kinnerton

---

[1] Neither Mr. Cutler nor Mr. Lane was at that time much known in
the surgical world ; but Mr. Lane's reputation as an anatomical teacher
naturally brought him—as it had done to his master, the elder Wilson—
some share of consulting surgical practice. A few years later, in his
letter to the Governors of St. George's declining to stand in opposition
to Mr. Tatum in 1840, he could say of himself that he had "been
entrusted by his professional brethren with many of the principal
operations in surgery ; " and this must, of course, have been in private
practice, for at that time Mr. Lane had no hospital appointment.

Street, about five minutes' walk from the hospital. The money was found by Brodie, and the school paid him interest on it, as a matter of course. Its distance from the hospital was its only drawback, otherwise it was well suited to the purpose; and its dissecting-room was, at that period at least, the best in London. The opening of this school of course increased the antagonism between "Lane's school" and the followers of Brodie, and for some time the board-room of the hospital was the scene of bitter and unseemly disputes, and men who were colleagues at the hospital were not on speaking terms.

The cause of contention ceased, when, on the foundation of St. Mary's Hospital, in 1845 or 1846, Mr. Lane removed his school there, leaving the Kinnerton Street school the only one connected with St. George's Hospital; and the relations of the Governors of the hospital towards each other became more friendly, so that the proceedings of the Board resumed their proper dignity and quiet.

I have not hesitated to express my opinion that, in the contest which first brought this painful dissension before the public, Brodie was in the wrong—that Mr. Lane was more entitled to the place to which he aspired than Mr. Cutler was, and that it would have been better for St. George's Hospital if it had secured the services of one so eminently qualified as an anatomist, a surgeon, and a teacher. But the whole weight of blame is seldom justly to be laid on one side in a quarrel of this sort, and I believe that the quarrel was aggravated and protracted by the bitterness and

violence of the language of Dr. Wilson and his
adherents, and that Brodie behaved with the dignity
which his position (and I may add his success in
securing the objects out of which the quarrel grew)
required. Little of Brodie's correspondence has been
preserved, but among the papers which the kindness
of the present Sir Benjamin Brodie entrusted to me
for perusal there is a bundle which relates to this
subject, and which fully bears out the view of the
matter given above.

The quarrel was carried on in the most unseemly
manner, by letters in the public papers, by pamphlets
both signed and unsigned, and by all the other arts of
popular agitation ; with which, however, Brodie had
nothing to do, and which, damaging as they were to
the prosperity and reputation of the hospital, cannot,
in fairness, be laid at his door.

When I joined the hospital as a student in 1848 the
fire which once blazed fiercely had gone out, and only
traditions of its heat remained. Sir Benjamin was
enjoying the well-deserved supremacy which he so
long exercised over the medical world, and his opponents had made their mark and obtained a fair measure
of success. Nor was it ever true, as the other party
said, that Brodie could carry everything before him at
St. George's and could, as some one (parodying a
classical anecdote) phrased it, " make his coach-horse
Surgeon to St. George's if he pleased ; " for in 1843,
not many years after Mr. Cutler's election, when the
then assistant, and lifelong friend of Brodie, Mr.
Charles Hawkins, the editor afterwards of his Works,

stood for the post of Assistant-Surgeon, he was defeated by Mr. H. C. Johnson, although nearly all Brodie's colleagues supported Mr. Hawkins's candidature.

The present seems a natural place for a short digression on the subject of elections on the medical staff of our hospitals : for there can be no doubt that the election of which we have been speaking exercised a great influence on Brodie's life, and is very important in forming a judgment of his character.

At that time, and for many years afterwards—in fact down to very recent times—the members of the staff were elected at St. George's by the votes of all the Governors. In order to be a Governor a person [1] must have subscribed a certain sum, and then have been elected by the Quarterly Court of Governors after the name has been suspended for a due time in the board-room. A few persons are also elected as Honorary Governors in recognition of services to the hospital : but in their case also the suspension of the name is required, and this is of importance in the question of elections, as it renders it impossible to create Governors for the occasion. In the election of Mr. Cutler the feeling ran high, and some influential persons supported Mr. Lane's candidature. Among Dr. Wilson's papers is a note from Sir Henry Halford promising his vote for Mr. Lane, and beside Dr. Wilson three other members of the staff sided with

---

[1] This person may technically be male or female : and there are a few lady Governors at St. George's ; but hitherto I am not aware that they have ever exercised their privileges.

Mr. Lane. Still the return of Mr. Cutler was so
strongly supported by Brodie and his numerous friends
and followers that "the issue was never doubtful,"[1] to
quote again from Dr. Dickinson's biographical notice.
It was very different in the case of Mr. H. C. Johnson's election in 1843. His opponent, Mr. Charles
Hawkins, commanded the support of most of the
staff, as well as that of Sir Benjamin Brodie; but Mr.
Johnson's personal popularity was very great, and Mr.
Hawkins's religious persuasion (he being a Roman
Catholic) was at that time an obstacle to the free action
of Brodie and his friends in his support. The contest
was hardly inferior in heat to that attending political
elections. The only two candidates were Mr. H. C.
Johnson and Mr. Charles Hawkins. Of the Governors
321 attended, of whom 169 voted for Johnson, and 152
for Hawkins. The keenness of the contest, and the extent to which canvassing had been carried, is shown by
the names of the great personages who were persuaded
to come down—the Duke of Cambridge, Archbishop
of Canterbury, Bishop of London, &c. Brodie did
not vote. This contest left many heartburnings and
quarrels behind it, which could not fail to injure the
hospital. It is much to the credit of Mr. Hawkins
that a repulse so mortifying as this did not extinguish
his interest in St. George's nor make him slacken in
using all his energies in its service. He was active in
that service up to the close of his long life, and was
for a long period the most prominent member of the
Board. Finally, another election took place, not

---

[1] See footnote 1, p. 116.

many years ago, in which a determined effort was made by some of the Governors to force on the medical staff a colleague whom they judged undesirable, founding that judgment on the way in which he had discharged the duties of some of the minor offices of the medical school. The attempt was defeated; but after so sharp a contest as to show clearly to all the friends of the institution the danger to which this method of election exposed it; and Mr. Charles Hawkins, impressed by this circumstance, as well as by his own former experience, proposed to the Board that they should resign their electoral functions into the hands of a large committee. The proposition was accepted, and the plan has hitherto worked well. The other permanent officials are, equally with the medical staff, elected by this committee. I believe this method is the best which can be adopted at such elections. It gives the acting medical staff a powerful voice in the selection of their future colleagues, since all the physicians and surgeons in charge of in-patients and all the consulting staff, who are in intimate relation with their old colleagues, are *ex-officio* members of the committee.[1] And it seems to me natural that the medical staff should have such a voice, for they know most about the candidates, they know best the qualifications required for the office, and they have the greatest interest in securing a good and

[1] The committee consists of the four Physicians, four Surgeons, the Consulting Physicians and Surgeons (a fluctuating number, averaging about six), the Vice-Presidents, Trustees and Treasurers (who are mostly laymen), the Senior Visiting Apothecary, and twenty-one other Governors, elected annually. Thus there is always a considerable preponderance of the lay or non-medical element.

efficient officer as their colleague. At the same time the presence of a preponderating non-medical element is an absolute security against jobbery or favouritism. Canvassing at these elections is prohibited, and this is another, and a very considerable, advantage. The canvassing of a large constituency is not only a painful task, very repulsive to the feelings of a gentleman, when the office he seeks is one for his own professional advancement, but it is also a very expensive proceeding, both in money and time. Thus an undue advantage is given to a rich over a poor man, and also to a man who has no practice over one who has made his mark, and whose time is already valuable. But the chief object is the exclusion of undue personal influence, such as was, I fear, exercised in Mr. Cutler's election. That Brodie's motives were pure we have no right now to deny, for we have not the materials for a judgment ; but it is, I think, probable that he was to some extent biassed, consciously or unconsciously, by that habitual exercise of influence and power at the hospital of which Dr. Dickinson speaks, and that he wished to retain the commanding position to which his services and his reputation had raised him. And every man, even one so highminded as Brodie, is tempted to think himself justified in preferring his friend, under such circumstances, to a stranger, still more to an opponent, and using his influence to the utmost. A strong committee, formed of independent men, versed in the daily business of the institution, is far less likely to succumb to such influence than a miscellaneous crowd who are dazzled by the glamour of a famous name.

VI

1834–1840

HONOURS AND PUBLIC SERVICES

Brodie made a Baronet—Becomes Examiner and Member of Council at the College of Surgeons— Reform in the examinations of the College—The new Charter of the College—Hunterian Oration of 1837—Foreign travel—Resigns at St. George's Hospital—Brodie as lecturer—The Brodie medal—Brodie in the country—Lady Brodie.

"There are . . . some remarkable examples of men earning a large income by a laborious profession, who have gained reputation in one of the sciences, or in some branch of literature, but these are very exceptional cases."—HAMERTON, "*The Intellectual Life*," p. 249.

IT was in the year 1834 that Brodie, who was now indisputably the leader of the surgical profession in London, and had been for some years Serjeant-Surgeon, received the recognition due to his eminence of a baronetcy. Not only was the honour unsought, but it is clear from the account of the matter in the Autobiography that it was undesired, at least at that time. Brodie, who was far more cautious than ambitious, hardly thought his pecuniary position sufficiently secure to support the hereditary title, in view of the possibility of his early death. But the subject had been before Lord **Grey's** mind when he **was in office,** at and for a short time after **the Reform** Bill, and his successor, Lord Melbourne, **took it up,** and applied to the King, who immediately assented, and the matter was settled. Sir Benjamin's reflections on his elevation are **worth** quoting : " Prosperous as I was in my **profession, I** had always felt that **I was** overworked, and **that what I gained** in income was counterbalanced **by the loss of** comfort. It had been my dream (it **would, I** doubt not, **have proved only a dream) that I would, when I** had **made some further provision for my** family, **retire from professional** practice, and resume **my** former pursuits **in physiology. But now** the case was altered. An hereditary rank, however small, without some independent fortune, **is** really an incumbrance, and **I** considered it rather as a duty **to those who were to** come after me not to leave them **in this** situation. Thus I was led **to** persevere **in my former course ;** and it was not until **three or four years** afterwards that, by affording myself a long vacation during the summer **and autumn, I** obtained **any** considerable relaxation from **my labours." Mr. Charles Hawkins adds a footnote on** this passage, **stating that Sir** Benjamin **Brodie's professional** income never **exceeded** £12,000 **a year. He** might have said £11,000, but has evidently **misread a** somewhat ill-written figure in one of the **fee-books.** These books **show** that his professional **income** was usually rather **below** than above £10,000, but of course his savings were all the **time** rapidly accumulating at compound interest—and interest was much higher then than now.

I think we may agree with the author of the above passage that the dream of retiring from practice would have proved a dream only. Fond as Brodie was of physiology and of scientific work, he appears to have been still more fond of practical surgery, and I cannot bring myself to believe that he would ever have abandoned the multiform interests, and the thousand pleasant ties of gratitude and mutual esteem, which are formed between the successful surgeon and his patients for any pleasures of research or speculation.

Brodie combined, in an unusual degree, success in practice with eminence in science ; but it seems to me inconceivable that he should ever have sacrificed the former to pursue the latter. In the " Psychological Inquiries" (vol. i. p. 326), he expresses forcibly his sense of the necessity, for perfect happiness, of living in the world, and keeping up our interest in its concerns, and in our fellow-men. His was an eminently practical mind, and he had so great vigour of constitution and such power of work, that he could find amid the engrossing calls of practice enough leisure for scientific and speculative pursuits. Even at the time of which we are now speaking, I find notes, amongst the papers kindly entrusted to me by the present holder of the title, of physiological experiments at which Mr. Cutler and other of his friends assisted him, and the speculations which resulted in his work on psychology must have been occupying his thoughts long before that work was issued.

Again, I do not think that Brodie was at all insensible to the pecuniary considerations which commonly prevent men who have once tasted success from quitting a career so honourable and so lucrative. Not that he was avaricious. Everything that I have ever heard of him, and all the records of his life, tend, I think, to show that he was far above a passion so sordid as the love of money for itself.[1] But the extreme care with which at all periods of his Autobiography he reckons up his income, the scrupulous accuracy with which his fee-books for over fifty years are kept,[2] and the frequent references to prudential considerations in all the great events of his life, show that he was equally far from the folly of despising money ; and I cannot bring myself to believe that he would ever have been guilty of the error which Sir Astley Cooper committed when he gave up practice, only to find himself so miserable in his idleness that he was fain to return to London. Doubtless Brodie had more resources in himself than Cooper had, but the result would very probably have been not very different. At any rate, he continued in practice till growing infirmities compelled his retirement.

---

[1] See Appendix I., Brodie on making money.

[2] The books in which he recorded his professional earnings commence in 1806, when he was twenty-three years old, with the modest sum of £140, chiefly derived from his work in the dissecting-room, and end in July, 1860, when his sight was beginning to fail, with the sum of £1,035 6s. received in fees during those six months. Every month is duly cast up and carried forward, and the amount derived from the fees of daily practice distinguished from the receipts from lectures, from examinations, and from his office as Serjeant-Surgeon. "In 1820," says the memoir in the *Lancet*, October 25, 1862, "he was already in the realisation of a handsome professional income." His fee-book for that year shows a total of £4,606 5s. 3d.

And now, in 1834, began his official connection with that great institution, the College of Surgeons, which owes its present position of influence and dignity mainly to the reforms which Brodie initiated, or rather which he, single-handed, effected. In those days the Court of Examiners was a close body. As each vacancy occurred, it was filled up by the votes of the Council, and from the Council themselves. In order, apparently, somewhat to modify this monopoly of the post of Examiner by the Councillors, it had been stipulated that the two Serjeant-Surgeons should be *ex-officio* members of the Court. Thus there were always two examiners who were responsible servants of the Crown, and not nominees of the Council, and in one case at least (that of Sir David Dundas, mentioned by Brodie) the Examiner was not even a member of the College.[1] It was under this rule that Sir Benjamin Brodie, on being appointed Serjeant-Surgeon, became an Examiner, and he held the position only as long as the rule remained in force. When the Serjeant-Surgeon ceased to be an *ex-officio* Examiner, under the provisions of the Charter of 1843, Brodie retired from the Court.

To the duties of this office he gave the same scrupulous care as he did to every duty which he undertook. Amongst his private papers I find some notes which show how much his mind was occupied

[1] Dundas, however, was objected to by the College as being only an apothecary, and I conclude, from Mr. South's account of the matter, that though he held the office of Examiner nominally, he did not attempt to perform its functions (see South, "The Craft of Surgery," pp. 287–8).

with the question of improving the method of examining and the qualifications of the candidates. At that period the qualifying examination was in ordinary cases entirely oral, and at the end of an hour's questions and answers the candidate was dismissed, "passed" or "referred back to his studies." But in some cases the result of the *vivâ voce* examination was indecisive, and the candidate was submitted to a written examination. Sir Benjamin took the trouble of analysing sixty-four of these written papers, being the whole number in a certain period of time, and his note (undated) is headed rather sarcastically, "Educational Statistics of one of the Learned Professions." I conjecture that its object was to show the necessity of a more liberal education, and sounder grounding in ordinary learning, before beginning medical studies, and thus to pave the way for the preliminary examination for the Fellowship which he afterwards introduced. His analysis shows that only forty out of the sixty-four candidates could spell properly, and that, out of fifty-six who were required to translate English prescriptions into Latin, only twenty did so without false concords, wrong spelling, or ungrammatical construction. On this question of the necessity of a liberal general education Brodie's views never varied ; and in principle I think no one would question their soundness, though I fear it must be admitted that the preliminary examination for the Fellowship (which has now been abolished) failed to secure the object it had in view. It imposed on the candidate the expense and delay of a few months' "coaching" in little bits of French, Latin, and algebra, but left him as unprovided with any useful knowledge of these branches of learning as it found him. Things have changed now, and no one is admitted to register as a medical student till he has passed some qualifying examination in letters; yet my own experience as an examiner at the College of Surgeons has convinced me that there is still much to be desired in the general education of our students; and that the proportion of those who spell badly, and still more of those who could not put four or five Latin words together decently, would be, if not so high as in those days, still far higher than it ought to be.

There are also among these papers several calculations of the average income derived from membership of the Court of Examiners. These calculations were, I fancy, somehow required for his project of introducing the anatomical and surgical examination for the Fellowship—an examination which has created a higher grade of members of the College, and has much raised its reputation, but was, and I believe still is, a source of loss rather than gain to its funds.

The Autobiography contains some reflections on medical examinations which are not only still worth study, but which contain principles that, if they had been more steadily kept in mind, would have obviated much mischief. In a work like this, intended as much for the general public as for medical men, I cannot go into details which would be both wearisome and unintelligible to the former; but the examination

question is one of general interest, and it cannot be
wholly unimportant, even to the non-medical reader, to
know how the examinations of so large a proportion
of our young men as the students of medicine form,
are conducted.

Under the old system of the College of Surgeons, as
I have said, there was no examination whatever in
general subjects at any period of the student's course,
and only one professional examination, at the end of
that course, in anatomy (including physiology) and
surgery. Medicine and midwifery were not touched
on, so that a man might obtain the diploma, and so be
entitled to practice without any knowledge of what
forms by far the greater part of the duties of a general
practitioner.[1] This was no doubt a most defective
system. It encouraged the idle to be idle till just before
the examination day approached, and then to attempt,
by a feverish process of " cram," to obtain a show of
knowledge sufficient to face the questions of the
examiners. Of course, the idiosyncrasies of these formidable persons had been studied, and their favourite
questions registered for the guidance of crammers and
crammed. These two great defects of the system
were at once apparent to Brodie, and are pointed out,
briefly but emphatically, in the Autobiography. "The
great objection to the *vivâ voce* examination is the
facility with which a student, having a good memory
and a clever tutor, may qualify himself for the ordeal
by cramming." . . . "It would be a great improve-

[1] In practice, however, most general practitioners had obtained the
license also of the Apothecaries' Hall or the College of Physicians.

ment on the present system if the examinations were
conducted at two distinct periods ; the one relating to
anatomy and physiology taking place when half the
period allotted to education was expired, and the other
at the termination of the whole. Further, without
giving up the *vivâ voce* examination altogether, a part
of the examination should always be conducted by
means of written papers."

The one merit which the old system had, was that
it kept the student at work (as far as he worked at all)
on all the topics of the examination till the end of his
period of study ; whilst at present he quits the dissecting-room as soon as he has passed the primary [1]
examination, and never re-enters it for purposes of
serious study in anatomy, whilst as for physiology he
has usually forgotten all the little he ever knew about
that science—the very groundwork of all scientific
medicine—before he presents himself for the final or
diploma examination.

Brodie saw also that the ordinary examination for
diplomas must necessarily be of quite a different
character from scholastic or competitive examinations.
"The utmost that can be expected of a young lawyer,
or physician, or surgeon, is that he should show that
he has laid such a foundation as may enable him to
profit by the opportunities of experience which may be
presented to him afterwards." Some writers, espe-

---

[1] It may be as well to note here for the information of non-medical
readers that the main divisions of the qualifying examination are—(1)
The preliminary, in general literature, before registration as a student ;
(2) the primary, in anatomy and physiology ; (3) the final, or diploma
examination.

cially in the public papers, speak as if the Colleges, when they license young men, guarantee their immediate fitness for all the emergencies of medicine and surgery. This would be absurd. They are no more fit to undertake the duties, say, of a hospital surgeon than a lieutenant who has just put on his uniform is to command a brigade. They have done no practice for themselves, and it is only by actual practice on one's own responsibility that one can ever be fitted for emergencies. But the youths who obtain their diplomas have to fill subordinate positions for long periods of time, during which they have the assistance and control of their seniors, and gradually acquire the necessary experience.

Brodie, however, perceived how much strength the College of Surgeons might acquire from the institution of a higher order of members, qualified by more advanced age, and a higher standard of examination, and for this purpose he devised the order of Fellows. The object of this institution was, in the words of its founder, "to insure the introduction into the profession of a certain number of young men who may be qualified to maintain its scientific character, and will be fully equal to its higher duties as hospital surgeons, teachers and improvers of physiological, pathological, and surgical science afterwards." And well, indeed, has this reform answered its object. It has raised the College of Surgeons from a status little higher than that of a City company to something more fitting its rank as one of the chief institutions of a great profession, and the exemplar of surgical education to the whole kingdom, and the examination for the Fellowship which Brodie introduced is now regarded as the most honourable surgical examination in Great Britain and perhaps in the world.

The creation of this new order of members necessitated a new Charter from the Crown, and this was obtained in the year 1843, mainly through the exertions of Sir Benjamin Brodie, and his influence with those who were then in power.

The new Charter made an enormous improvement in every department of the College. On the old system members of Council were alone eligible as examiners, and when a vacancy occurred the senior member not on the Court of Examiners was elected almost as a matter of course. Brodie notes as a remarkable exception that the two seniors were passed over to bring Lawrence into the Court somewhat before his usual "turn." The old routine of the examinations was followed from generation to generation, the examiners held office for life, and used to exercise their right as long as they could sit at the table—so that it is recorded of Sir William Blizard, who died over ninety years of age, that he was examining within six weeks of his death [1]—and there was no control whatever over the acts or the expenditure of the Council from

[1] Brodie in his Hunterian Oration, delivered shortly after Sir William's death, gives a pleasant notice of his venerable predecessor, and of his respect for the College, and for all that was ancient. "Those who are much advanced in life," says the Orator "generally form a lower estimate of the march of knowledge than those who are younger ; and this, I doubt not, is to be attributed in great measure to their knowing less of what has been gained ; but it is to be attributed also, in part, to their knowing more of what has been lost" (vol. i. p. 461).

public opinion, or any other authority except the shadowy and nominal supremacy of the Privy Council.

The state of things in old days was described to the governing body of the College itself by one of its members, whom I have had occasion to mention casually on a former page—the elder John Gunning, of St. George's Hospital—in the following vigorous terms : " You have a theatre for your lectures, a room for a library, a committee-room for your Court, a large room for the reception of your communities, together with the necessary accommodation for your clerk. . . . Your theatre is without lectures, your library-room, without books, is converted into an office for your clerk, and your committee-room is become his parlour, and is not always used even in your common business, and when it is thus made use of it is seldom in a fit and proper state." This is not the libel of some enemy, but occurs in a speech which Mr. Gunning, as Master, made to the Court on the termination of his year of office in 1789–90. It is satisfactory to be assured, on the authority of Mr. South, that " the reproof was taken in good part by the Company, and a committee was appointed to inquire into the truth of the allegations, and a series of resolutions were ultimately embodied reforming the more flagrant abuses." [1]

This was in the days of the old Company, which ceased to exist a few years afterwards, in consequence of some technical breaches of their Act of Incorpora-

[1] South, " Memorials of the Craft of Surgery in England." Edited by D'Arcy Power, 1886, pp. 286, 287.

tion. The Royal College of Surgeons in London
was constituted by Act of Parliament in 1800; but
it retained some of the characters of a City company
until 1821, when it received a supplemental charter
from George IV., and when its Court of Masters
and Governors was replaced by a Council with
a president and vice-presidents.

Brodie's great service to the College, and to the
profession and the public through the College, was
that he enlarged the constitution of this original
Royal College of Surgeons by the creation of a
higher order of members, under the title of Fellows,
and by the introduction of a higher examination as
their qualification for that dignity. I am myself disposed to regard his work as imperfect, in that it left
the whole power not only of administration, but also
of initiation—in fact all possible power—in the hands
of the Council, thus enabling these twenty-four
individuals to take any step they please, however
profoundly it may change the relations of the
College to the public, or to the profession, not
only without the sanction, but even, conceivably,
in opposition to the declared wishes of the body
which they represent, and by whom they were
elected. But, whether I am right or wrong in
this opinion, there can be no doubt that the present
constitution of the College is a very great improvement on that which it replaced, and that Brodie did
a most important service to the public and to the
medical profession by procuring the new Charter of
the College of Surgeons of England in the year 1843.

HONOURS AND PUBLIC SERVICES

In February, 1837, he delivered the Hunterian Oration at the College of Surgeons. It was a subject which must have interested him, both from his connection with the family of his great predecessor at St. George's and from the consciousness, which he could not but have felt, that he was the only distinguished surgeon who up to that time had succeeded in following Hunter by combining the study of science with the practice of surgery, though Sir Everard Home had no doubt attempted the same task, but not with success.

Interesting as the whole speech is, it is at its termination that it rises to eloquence in setting forth the delights of philosophical study to the student of medicine, as follows : " Is it not an advantage in any profession to have some object which may engage the attention beyond the drudgery of professional practice ; to which the mind may turn with delight as a relaxation from severer duties, to which it may retreat as a refuge in the hour of anxiety and disappointment ? Everywhere around us—in the air, in the waters, on the surface, and even in the deep, dark caves in the recesses of the earth—we recognise the operation of that mighty principle which animates the universe. . . . A boundless field is open to our observation ; and whatever part of it we explore we discover subjects of admiration not inferior to those which are presented to the astronomer. . . . It is in this part of the creation more than in any other that we discern the manifestations of the Creator. In the history and structure of individual animals we

find marks of intelligence, power, and benevolence
beyond what our minds can measure; while the
uniformity of the design which pervades the whole
system affords an unanswerable argument in favour
of the uniformity of the cause in which it had its
origin" (vol. i. p. 464).

In this year also—1837—Brodie experienced for
the first time the delightful novelty of a tour abroad.
It seems strange to us in these days, when it is so
easy to cross the Channel, and when we get to the
great cities of France, Germany, or Italy in less time
than it took in Brodie's youth to get to Newcastle,
that a man so active, so rich, and so alive to
foreign ideas as he was should have lived to
over fifty years of age without ever having
been out of England. But Brodie tells us that,
though he could read French and Italian with ease,
he could not speak any language except his own;
and in those days, if it was not actually necessary
to speak the languages, yet the traveller who was
limited to his own tongue was at a great disadvantage,
as well as being subject to greatly increased expense.
"It is worthy of notice," says the Autobiography,
"that formerly the speaking French was far from
being a frequent accomplishment. Sir Joseph Banks
never conversed with foreigners without the aid of
an interpreter, and I have understood that Mr.
Canning did not acquire the habit of speaking
French until he was, as it were, compelled to do
so by becoming the Secretary of State for the
Foreign Department." All Brodie's French and

other scientific visitors seem to have had to speak English to him. Yet Brodie was ahead of his contemporaries in possessing a literary knowledge of what were then the two chief continental languages ; for German had not yet attained the scientific or medical importance which it now has. And no doubt he would have made himself personally familiar with the schools and with the medical and scientific celebrities of the Continent, but for the unflagging energy with which he prosecuted his professional advancement in London.

On the present occasion he made a short tour in Normandy, and then resided for a month in Paris, being accompanied by his wife and daughter. He was, of course, warmly received by the scientific and medical celebrities of Paris, most of whom he had already known in London. He only once re-visited Paris, and when he wrote his Autobiography in 1857 he tells us that he had only been once in Switzerland and once in Italy as far as Milan.

In January, 1840, he resigned the office of Surgeon to St. George's, after filling it for eighteen years. For the fourteen previous years he was nominally Assistant-surgeon ; but, as we have seen, he was really discharging the duties rather of a full surgeon than of an assistant, during pretty nearly the whole period, so that his period of hospital service may be reckoned as thirty-two years. In thus resigning, he tells us, he " was influenced by various considerations." One, and doubtless the most important, was his sense of the necessity of diminishing the amount of his labours; and after thirty-two years of such work at the hospital as few men have ever done, he might well feel that he had earned the right, at the age of fifty-seven, to work for himself in the future. But I do not doubt his sincerity when he says that he had long formed the resolution that he would not have it said of himself, what he had often heard said of others, that he had retained a situation of such importance and responsibility when from age or indifference he had ceased to be fully equal to its duties. And I have no doubt he is equally sincere in saying that he felt it to be selfish to stand in the way of intelligent and deserving juniors waiting for the appointment, from which he had already obtained all he could desire, as far as his mere worldly interests were concerned. It was worthy of Brodie's high character to look in this generous spirit at a question which many others hardly less exalted than he was in professional rank have judged so differently.[1] He was succeeded in the office of Surgeon by Mr. Walker, who, however, only held that post for three years, when he died, and Mr. Tatum succeeded him.

We must allow that Brodie's action in this matter is very much to his credit for disinterestedness. The post of Surgeon to St. George's was at that time a lucrative one, and Brodie, as I believe, was not insensible to pecuniary matters, though more from family considerations than from a love of money in itself; he had ample vigour, and was fond of the

---

[1] See above as to Mr. R. Keate, p. 52.

work, so that he tells us that for a long time after his resignation he never passed the hospital without a feeling of regret that his work there was over. And his love for the institution itself must have tended to bind him to its continued service, as it did induce him to deliver annually short courses of lectures to the students in the winter session, "generally selecting for his subject some one class of disease, and giving a more detailed history of his own experience than was possible in an ordinary course of surgical lectures."

I regret that these lectures had come to an end just before I joined the school, so that I never heard this great master of his art lecture clinically. But I believe that he was an admirable lecturer, clear, forcible, and full of matter, and the evident pleasure which he had in imparting knowledge, both by formal lectures and by the more conversational instruction given in the wards, showed that he had a talent for that part of a hospital surgeon's duty, while the grateful recollections of the many distinguished surgeons who were his pupils and successors testify to the worth of his teaching and his eminence as a clinical instructor. A well-informed writer in the *Lancet*,[1] who seems to have attended his lectures, thus speaks of his powers as a lecturer : "As a teacher, he was always distinguished for the value of the *matter* he had to communicate. Those who heard him in the early part of his career say that he was then energetic rather than polished ; that he appeared to struggle with the

[1] Vol. ii., 1862, p. 456.

weight and mass of facts he had stored up in his mind.
But in later years his delivery was fluent and perfect. No man in his profession could deliver
himself more readily or more elegantly than Sir
B. Brodie."

And Sir Henry Acland [1] thus describes Brodie's
manner as a lecturer : "None who heard him can
forget the graphic yet artless manner in which, sitting
at his ease, he used to describe minutely what he had
himself seen and done under circumstances of difficulty, and what under like circumstances he would
again do, or would avoid. His instructions were
illustrated by valuable pathological dissections which
during many years he had amassed and which he
gave during his lifetime to his hospital."

He expressed the attachment which he felt for
the hospital, as follows, in an address at which I
remember to have been present : "I trust I need not
assure you of the great interest which I still feel in the
prosperity of the hospital itself, and in the reputation
of the medical school which is connected with it. It
would indeed be strange if it were otherwise. It was
here that I began the study of that profession, the
practice of which has been the main object of my
life. For whatever knowledge I have been able to
acquire, for whatever advantages have accrued to me
professionally, for these I am more or less indebted to
my connection with this institution; which is, moreover, associated in my mind with many agreeable
recollections of friendships with my colleagues and

---

[1] Biographical sketch of Sir B. Brodie, p. 21.

pupils—of the interesting pursuits, the hopes and fears and aspirations of my early life." [1]

His numerous friends and admirers naturally took the occasion of Brodie's retirement from the hospital as an opportunity for putting into permanent form the appreciation and gratitude of the profession and public for his eminent services to the art and practice of surgery. Hence the origin of the " Brodie Medal," which was finally presented at a public dinner at Willis's Rooms on August 3, 1843, Sir C. M. Clarke in the chair. "The medal," says the *Lancet*, September 2, 1843, " is a fine specimen of the art, by Mr. Wyon, of the Royal Mint. On the obverse it presents the bust of Sir B. Brodie, and on the reverse a female figure, emblematical of medicine, in the attitude of kneeling to trim the Hygeian lamp. Over the design is the appropriate motto from Lucretius, ' E tenebris tantis tam clarum extollere lumen qui potuisti.'"

Of Brodie's speech on this occasion Dr. (afterwards Sir Charles) Locock said it was "really and truly beautiful, intensely affecting, simply earnest and true, doing honour to his head and his heart. There was no affectation ; it was the honest effusion of a grateful mind for such a public tribute to his merits."

Of the medal Lady Brodie wrote to her son: " It is indeed a superb work of art. The likeness is perfect, and I cannot find a fault with it. The reverse is beautifully executed but terribly ob-scure. I should have preferred your selected motto from Bacon—nevertheless, altogether I am gratefully delighted."

Amongst the papers which Mr. Charles Hawkins gave to the present Sir Benjamin Brodie is a letter from Lord Denman, dated from Westminster Hall, January 31, 1844, acknowledging the gift of a copy of the Brodie medal, in these terms : " I beg leave to assure you, and the Committee for preparing the Brodie testimonial, that your beautiful memorial could not have been bestowed on any one who could prize it more highly. Let me add that I am gratified by the motives which you assign for showing me this kindness—my near connection with eminent members of the medical profession, and the place which I have had the good fortune to reach in my own. But you perhaps are not aware that one of those eminent men is Sir Benjamin Brodie himself, whom I am proud to call my near kinsman, and my friend through life. In our early days we were taught—and have found it true—that all honourable and beneficial pursuits are closely allied, and promote the credit and usefulness of each other."

This seems an appropriate place to speak of Sir Benjamin Brodie's life in the country and in his own family.

At the time when Brodie was offered a baronetcy, he considered that his landed property was not of sufficient extent to warrant his acceptance of the honour ; nevertheless, he had previously invested a considerable portion of his savings in the purchase of some farms in the parishes of Boxford and Preston, near the town of Bury St. Edmunds, in the county of Suffolk.

Landed property in those days was considered the most important form of investment, and it is not surprising that he should have considered his position as not being sufficiently secured in the world to enable him to accept and maintain the hereditary title until he had acquired a certain amount of land to hold with it. The investment appears to have been at that time a good one, and he continued for some years after to add to his property in Suffolk. During the more active period of his professional life Brodie had never been absent from London for more than a few weeks in the year. His house at Hampstead, at that time in the country, had served his purpose, and for some nine years he had rented it, and had been in the habit of residing there during the summer and autumn months, driving in and out every day.

In 1837, feeling that he had a right to consult his own comfort a little more than he had done, and that some relaxation from his labours was required, he decided to purchase a property nearer to London, and Broome Park, in the village of Betchworth in Surrey, being at that time for sale, he became the owner of that estate.

It was not without some misgivings, both on his own part and on that of his wife, that he fixed upon a house at such a distance, some twenty-four miles from London, and as he desired to be in the country from Saturday to Monday through the summer and autumn, the long drive was considered by Lady Brodie at first as an insuperable difficulty. But the beauties of the spot, and the fact that he had evidently set his heart upon it, overcame her scruples, and in November, 1837, he became the purchaser.

Though he himself, as he says, had seldom suffered from illness, yet he was scarcely strong enough for the large amount of work he had to do, and his health would no doubt have failed altogether if he had not taken this step. Lady Brodie's health, moreover, had been for some time anything but satisfactory, and this also probably increased the necessity of spending more time away from London.

Of his wife we have said up to the present time but little, and some few words respecting her who for forty-five years shared his joys and sorrows, and of whom it might be said, "The world would lose, if such a wife as you should vanish unrecorded," may well be introduced here.

She was, as we have seen, the third daughter of Serjeant Sellon, by his wife Charlotte Dickinson. Her brother-in-law, M. Regnault, died in Paris only last year at the advanced age of ninety-nine years, having, as it was said, outlived two empires, two monarchies, and two republics. Her grandfather, the Rev. William Sellon, was for many years rector of St. James's, Clerkenwell. He came of an old Protestant family, and his granddaughter inherited these opinions. She was a very zealous Evangelical, combining therewith extreme kindness of heart and a genuine desire to do good to all around her. Her letters to her children bring out her religious opinions in a very marked degree, and show how large a place in her heart their spiritual as well as their bodily welfare occupied. She possibly did not meet with that entire union of opinion in her husband which she probably desired. But, though Sir Benjamin was not so demonstrative on theological subjects, on which no doubt he had thought for himself, and possibly arrived at his own conclusions, her affection and devotion to him, as appears in all her letters, is most touching, and show that her life was truly one with his. Though at first she had her doubts as to the wisdom of purchasing Broome Park—or, as it was formerly called, Tranquil Dale—she became much attached to the place, and indeed it was a beautiful spot. In a letter to her son at Balliol announcing the purchase, she says, " It is delightfully situated, and contains within itself every species of country pleasures. It is not quite to my taste in some respects, not having extended prospect enough, which renders it a place not capable of improvement, but it is lovely as a *home* park, and immediately on going out of the gate the scene is charming—three miles from Dorking, three from Reigate. The little beautiful village adjoins close by." The estate, which included a home farm attached to the park, consisted of some 450 acres.

Here many pleasant days were spent ; for though Sir Benjamin had not, as he says, any taste for what are called country pursuits—shooting or hunting—nevertheless, the management of the place, the cultivation of the gardens, and the planting of many trees and shrubs, which are now better known than they were then, afforded much employment and pleasure.

The grounds included two lakes or ponds, and here were planted azaleas, rhododendrons, and other things which delight in moisture, and under the care of Lady Brodie and her gardener flourished extremely. The hill also was planted with larch-trees and underwood, and if the return for the outlay has been long postponed, at least their elegant and pleasing appearance has added to the beauty of that portion of the range which is crowned by the clump of trees known as the "Betchworth Beeches," and which form a landmark on the summit.

Before their arrival at Broome, the neighbouring hamlet of Brockham possessed neither church nor school. The want of these was greatly felt, and Lady Brodie set herself to supply the difficiency, and the now flourishing school at Brockham, which was opened in 1838, owes its existence mainly to her exertions. The church there also was built in 1843, with stone dug on the estate and given for that purpose.

Cricket matches in the park, school feasts, and other entertainments to the people in the village often took place, and when we see that fifty children of the Brockham School had provided for them "half a round of beef, sirloin ditto, two legs of mutton, plenty of potatoes, bread, beer, toast-and-water, with nine apple pies in dairy pans," it does not appear that the hospitality was sparingly dispensed.

Many distinguished friends were here entertained, Lord Brougham and Lord Denman, who came in 1838, being amongst the first.

Here, too, in 1845, during a Christmas visit, Lord Selborne met the lady who afterwards was to become his wife. She was the daughter of, at that time Admiral, afterwards Earl Waldegrave, and sister of the wife of the Rev. William Brodie, whose marriage had occurred a year previously.

VII

1840–1854

MANY-SIDED ACTIVITY

Personal appearance and professional relations—Presidency of Royal
Medical and Chirurgical Society — Papers on Quackery and
Homœopathy—Brunel's Case—The Chambers-Seymour Scandal
at St. George's Hospital—The Western Medical and Surgical
Society—Death of Sir R. Peel—Ethnological Society.

"Humani nil a me alienum puto."—Ter.

WE have now arrived at the culmination of
Brodie's professional career ; and I think
this will be an appropriate place to endeavour to give
some impression of his personal appearance, of his
teaching and method of practice, and his relations to
his patients and his professional brethren.

Sir Benjamin Brodie's personal appearance corre-
sponded well to the idea which I have endeavoured in
these pages to give of his character and his habits.
His features are admirably portrayed in the picture by
Watts, taken about two years before his death, which
the present inheritor of his name and title has been so

kind as to photograph for this volume. They were not, perhaps, strictly handsome, but no one could deny that they were striking. Keen grey eyes, a mobile and sensitive mouth, and facial muscles which followed all the movements of one of the most active of minds, lent to the countenance a charm and an impressiveness to which no stranger could be insensible. His frame was slight and small ; but there was nothing of weakness in it, and its movements were vigorous and even brusque, such as are habitual to a man whose whole life is passed in constant activity. Though we hear a good deal in his early days of fits of indisposition, it is evident that these were only the result of overwork, of driving the machine at a pace beyond human powers—not of any organic weakness in the machine itself. His manner was decided—sometimes perhaps somewhat abrupt—that of a man whose mind penetrated at once to the essence of the matter before him, and who had no time to waste on non-essential points : but it always indicated the truest kindness and sympathy, and the poor and the young never failed to find a friend in the great surgeon.

I must now speak of Brodie as a teacher and as a practitioner.

First for a very few words about his published works, other than those of which more detailed notice is taken elsewhere.

If this book were intended for medical readers only, I should have been bound to give a much more extended notice of Brodie's surgical writings than I think appropriate on the present occasion.

Especially should I have had to discuss the great work on " Diseases of the Urinary Organs," which had almost as important a part in promoting the progress of surgery as that on " Diseases of the Joints," and on which Brodie's reputation as a surgeon and as a surgical teacher rests almost equally. But such a discussion could not be adequately carried on without a thorough investigation of the surgical literature of our own and other countries in the earlier part of the present century, which would be both wearisome and unintelligible to the public ; and it would also be largely versed in details only fit for medical men ; and I therefore will not attempt it. Suffice it to say that this work, though I think it is admittedly inferior to that on diseases of the joints in originality, because its subject had been much better worked out by previous authors than diseases of the joints had been, shares in the other excellences of that great treatise. It is emphatically a practical book, resting on the firm foundation of pathology, and supported in all its reasonings and conclusions by the author's immense experience and unfailing accuracy of observation. It effected, I believe, an improvement, which we can now hardly estimate, in the treatment of a class of diseases extremely common, very fatal in their results if neglected or illtreated, and which were then, even more than they are now, favourable subjects for quacks and ignoramuses to practise on, to the ruin of the health and life of their victims.

Closely connected with this work—forming in fact a portion of its later editions—is the paper in the

"Medico-Chirurgical Transactions" which records the great progress in the treatment of Stone by means of crushing—or lithotrity—which owed so much to Brodie's ready appreciation of Civiale's teaching and practice, and to the zeal and ingenuity which he showed in improving the instruments and elaborating the details of the process. Brodie had, of course, nothing to do with the invention of lithotrity—this was due to French surgeons. And the perfection of the invention, by which the whole stone is removed at one sitting, litholapaxy, was devised by Bigelow, an American surgeon. But it was Brodie who popularised the method in England, and by so doing chiefly contributed to the ready reception of an operation which has robbed what was one of the deadliest diseases that afflict humanity of nearly all its terror. This will remain to all time one of Brodie's greatest claims to public gratitude.

In his private practice he earned, not only the gratitude, but the warm affection of many who owed life and health to his wise judgment and his unceasing care.

Those who live in the present day, when specialists exist for every form of disease, can scarcely perhaps be fully aware of the estimation in which Brodie was held.

He was consulted by patients of all ages and upon almost every conceivable form of accident or disease, and the variety of the entries in his case-books, many of which are still preserved, serve to show the position which he held, not only in Surgery, but as a real "Master of Medicine."

When at the time of the publication of the "Pick-wick Papers," Miss Mitford desired to impress upon some of her friends their extraordinary popularity, she wrote, "All the boys and girls talk his fun—the boys in the street; and yet those who are of the highest taste like it the most. Sir Benjamin Brodie takes it to read in his carriage between patient and patient; and Lord Denman studies 'Pickwick' on the Bench while the jury are deliberating." Such was the success of Pickwick; but it shows well the position of Brodie. It is curious that two first cousins should have been considered typical of the medical and legal professions.

Of the numerous gifts he received one or two may perhaps be mentioned.

Soon after the death of the Duchess of Kent the Queen forwarded to him a pair of vases "which Her Majesty chose for him among the ornaments in the Duchess of Kent's drawing-room at Clarence House, believing that by one whose care and skill had been so much valued by Her Majesty's beloved mother such a remembrance would be prized." Her Majesty also sent him portraits of herself and the late lamented Prince Consort, and these marks of Royal favour are much valued by his descendants.

Of gifts from private friends, that of Samuel Rogers, the poet, may be referred to. Rogers, with his friend Moore, was always a welcome and a very frequent guest at Savile Row. He was a true and most grateful friend and his gift (a silver gilt vase) on which is inscribed "A Tribute of gratitude for so long a friendship and for so many generous and noble efforts to serve him on his journey through life from Samuel Rogers to Sir Benjamin C. Brodie, Bart., &c." bears testimony of that feeling which is elsewhere frequently expressed in letters.

A curious case of an anonymous gift may be recorded. A small box was one day left at Sir Benjamin's house. This on being opened was found to contain a jade vase set with rubies, apparently of Eastern workmanship and of considerable value. It bore no name, nor any mark by which the donor might be discovered ; but inside was a small paper on which was inscribed the words, " For an unrequited service." Sir Benjamin never knew who sent it or what service it repaid.

The donor must probably long ere this have passed away, but the vase remains a silent tribute to the skill and kindness of the distinguished surgeon and a memorial of the gratitude of some unknown person who had experienced them.

Sir Benjamin never encouraged his patients to imagine themselves worse than they really were, and such as were inclined to do so were not unfrequently treated in a somewhat brusque manner. A story is told of a gentleman who had met with some slight accident in the hunting field in Ireland, who had applied for relief to various surgeons in that country and without success. At length he came to London to consult Sir Benjamin. He drove up in a carriage and with no little difficulty landed himself inside the house at Savile Row, his leg being carefully strapped up. Brodie undid the bandage and examined the limb and after a short time left the room. On his return, the patient desired that the bandages might be replaced and that his carriage might be called. Brodie, however, remarking that this was unnecessary as he intended him to walk home and adding that he had taken upon himself to dismiss the carriage, called his servant and requested him to assist the patient down the steps and then to leave him to find his own way home. This was done with the most beneficial results, as the gentleman recovered the use of his limb and .suffered no ill effects from his accident.

A rather amusing anecdote used to be told by Sir Benjamin. He was visiting one day a patient of his who resided in a fashionable part of London. Just as he was leaving the house the owner requested him to see an old and valued servant of his who for some time past had not been at all well. The servant—a butler —was sent for and it was immediately apparent that too good living and too little exercise were responsible to a very great extent for the retainer's indisposition. Brodie having examined him prescribed some medicine for him and then proceed to lay down a few regulations respecting his diet. He told him he must be very moderate in what he ate and drank, careful not to eat much at a time or late at night, &c. Above all, no spirituous liquors could be allowed, malt liquor especially being poison to his complaint. Whilst these directions were being given the butler's face grew longer and longer, and at the end he exclaimed, "And pray, Sir Benjamin, who is going to compensate me for the loss of all these things." The idea that

restored health could be in any way a sufficient com
pensation for the denial of such enjoyments did not
appear to have entered his head.

One of Brodie's professional excellences was the
regularity and fulness with which he communicated
his opinion to the many medical men who sent
patients to him for his advice. He seems throughout
his career to have been punctilious in his attention to
this amongst the many other calls on his time. The son
of one of these practitioners, Mr. Fowke, the secretary
of the British Medical Association, has been so kind as
to let me see some letters, and fragments of letters, of
this class, which Brodie sent to his father, Mr. John
Fowke, of Wolverhampton. They all treat of cases
in private practice, and they are all marked by Brodie's
usual lucidity of exposition and sound common sense.
The cases are various, and yet all of them belong to
classes in which the surgical profession was indebted to
him for real progress in pathological knowledge, and in
sound treatment founded thereon, such as mammary
tumours, scirrhus, serocystic tumour, joint disease,
spinal caries, varicose veins. Perhaps I may be
excused for quoting what Brodie says to his consul-
tant on the latter subject ; for it is interesting to note
how far more efficient is surgery now than it was
then, even in the hands of so enterprising a surgeon
as Brodie : " In cases of very bad varicose veins, I have
sometimes known the patient to derive benefit from
being kept in bed, with the heel a little elevated and a
blister kept open over the dilated veins, by means of
the savine cerate. But this is a painful process, and a

tedious process, occupying several successive weeks, and I never recommend it, except in very bad cases, when the patient suffers a great deal from the disease. I certainly do not mean to suggest it in the present instance. It appears to me that Mr. S. will derive much relief from the application of a flannel bandage, which after all affords a better support than any other bandage, and I should believe also that nothing else can, with prudence, be recommended to him. October 20, 1825." In the seventy years which have elapsed since this was written, chloroform and antiseptics have revolutionised the surgical treatment of many diseases, and amongst others have enabled surgeons, acting on the suggestion of my late friend, Mr. John Marshall, to dissect out even the most extensive clusters of dilated veins, without any pain and with very little danger ; and so to substitute an effective and immediate remedy for the tedious, painful, and ineffective one here suggested by Brodie. But while we confess that we moderns are indebted for this to anæsthetics and antiseptics, we should not forget that the operation was in use twenty centuries before either had been heard of, and is described by Celsus so accurately and minutely that one who had never seen it done could practice it from his description. True, indeed, it is, that but for anæsthetics and antiseptics it could not be practised now. Modern sensitiveness to pain would not endure it without the one, and the modern respect for human life would not tolerate the mortality which would follow, without the other.

After Brodie's resignation of his hospital appointment in 1840, he continued for some years his connection with the College of Surgeons as an examiner as well as member of the Council, and with his large practice, his constant occupation on physiological and scientific research, and his duties as Serjeant-Surgeon, he might well have pleaded that he had no time for more labour. But this was not Brodie's way. His mind was as active as his body, and both seemed to seek refreshment rather in variety of occupation than in repose ; and he appears never to have cooled in that affection for scholarship and the higher walks of literature which led him at first to regret and almost to rebel against his abandonment of literary for medical studies (see p. 29). So that the time which he saved from the laborious duties of a hospital surgeon was not given up to repose, nor consumed in the pursuit of fortune, but was used for activities of various kinds. One product of this mental labour was his " Psychological Inquiries," which were published anonymously in 1854—at least the First Part—but which must have occupied him for many years previously. But of this work I shall speak in a separate chapter.

Another outlet for his energies was the Royal Medical and Chirurgical Society. As we have seen, Brodie joined this Society early in his life, having been elected a Fellow in 1813, and his first contribution to its " Transactions " was read in that year, but must have been written earlier. He continued active in the service of the Society (or rather in the service of surgical science through the Society) almost down to the time of his death, for his most recent contribution to the "Transactions" is in the year 1861, in the form of a letter commenting on a paper on asphyxia—a subject on which, as we have seen, he had worked much and thought profoundly. Many of Brodie's papers in the grand series of "Medico-Chirurgical Transactions" are still standard authorities on the subjects of which they treat—such as diseases of the joints, varicose veins, injuries of the brain, chronic abscess of bone, lithotrity. Brodie was elected President of the Society (a biennial office) in 1839, so that he was in office at the time of his retirement from St. George's Hospital, and he forms an exception to the general rule in that his active work as a contributor continued long after the period of his presidency had passed. It must be remembered, however, that he became President earlier in life than most of his successors in that office. In the *Lancet*, vol. ii., 1862, p. 457, we read: "During the entire term of his presidency of the Royal Medical and Chirurgical Society we believe that he was not absent on a single occasion, and this is no small praise to a surgeon in his extensive and laborious practice. But it was after the reading of a paper that he was particularly great. Acting up to his axiom, that the debates in the Society constituted its most important and interesting feature, he always encouraged discussion. . . . Few of those who had the pleasure of hearing him will forget with what precision he spoke, how completely he kept *ad rem*, and how easily he brought his vast experience, and that, too, without preparation, to bear upon the production of the author, whoever it might be. . . . From the period of his presidency may be dated the remarkable prosperity of the Medical and Chirurgical Society, and this is mainly attributable, we believe, to the mode in which he fostered and protected discussion."

It was at this period of his many-sided activity that Brodie wrote the interesting and amusing paper on "Quacks and Quackery," which was published in the *Quarterly Review* for December, 1842. This short paper will well repay the time expended on its perusal to any one of moderate intelligence, whether a medical man or not. Beside the great merits of perfect clearness and perfect common sense which all Brodie's writings possess, it has that of humour, which he was usually prevented from exhibiting by the nature of the subjects which he was treating. But that Brodie had a keen sense of humour may be inferred from what is said by one who knew him well—Sir Henry Acland—who thus speaks in his obituary notice in the *Lancet* : " Those who knew him only as a man of business would little suspect the playful humour which sparkled by his fireside—the fund of anecdote, the harmless wit, the simple pleasures of his country walk."

His account of the " tar-water" theory patronised by Berkeley, the great philosopher, whom he took as his guide and exemplar ; of Perkins's system of "metallic tractors " (something analogous to which our own scientific age has witnessed), and of Dr. Haygarth's exposure of it ; of the "shampooing" which in its day was as fashionable as its congener "massage" now is ; of St. John Long ("that ruthless quack," as he is elsewhere called); of the "brandy and salt" which was widely believed in when I was young ; of homœopathy and hydropathy, which still continue to be to some extent lucrative, is as lively and as humorous as any one could desire, whilst the summary which he gives of each system is as accurate as if it were drawn up by one of its advocates.

But the great merit of the article lies in its conclusions. Brodie was too acute a philosopher and too experienced a man of the world to believe in either the desirability or the possibility of extirpating quackery by positive enactments. Quoting Lady Mary Wortley Montagu, as expressing his own opinion, he says of quackery, "I attribute it to the fund of credulity which is in all mankind. We have no longer faith in miracles and relics, and therefore with the same fury run after recipes and physicians. The same money which three hundred years ago was given for the health of the soul is now given for the health of the body, and by the same sort of persons—women and half-witted men. In the countries where they have shrines and images quacks are despised, and monks and confessors find their account in managing the hopes and fears which rule the actions of the multitude."

And here I may notice, though out of its chronological order, the short paper on homœopathy which was published not much more than a year before his death in *Fraser's Magazine* for September, 1861, as an admirable judgment on a controversy which still has a certain amount of vitality ; for there are still persons of intelligence in other matters who profess their faith in this so-called "system," qualified practitioners who are not ashamed to practise it, and hospitals founded ostensibly for homœopathic treatment. And all this in spite of there being no intelligible principles on which the so-called system could rest, except such as are too absurd to be really believed in by any man even moderately acquainted with medicine, and no proof whatever of any benefit derived from its practice. The very name is an imposture as implying that diseases are cured by the artificial production of similar diseases, which has been proved a thousand times to be either a falsehood or the delusion of gross ignorance, while the other so-called "principle," that medicines gain in power by dilution or trituration, is too ridiculous to be worthy of argument.[1]

But in the paper before us will be found, in the space of seven octavo pages, a lucid and convincing

[1] Brodie says in this paper : "The doses of medicine administered by ordinary practitioners are represented to be very much too large. It is unsafe to have recourse to them unless reduced to an almost infinitesimal point ; not only to the millionth, but sometimes even to the billionth of a grain. Now observe what this means. Supposing one drop of liquid medicine to be equivalent to one grain, then, in order to obtain the millionth part of that dose, you must dissolve that drop in thirteen gallons of water and administer only one drop of that solution ; while, in order to obtain the billionth of a grain, you must dissolve the aforesaid drop in 217,014 hogsheads of water." A deceased friend of my own, an accomplished mathematician and astronomer, used to say that a dilution, actually prescribed in homœopathic books, would require a sphere of water reaching from here to the nearest fixed star, to contain a drop of the solution—and I believe that he meant it seriously.

account of the causes which have originated, and still keep up so gross a delusion. First, of course, is the love of novelty, that fruitful mother of all quackeries "in dress, and gait, and e'en devotion." And in this connection Sir Benjamin wisely observes that the members of the medical profession had at first no prejudice against the new system; for "the fault of the profession, for the most part, lies in the opposite direction. They are too much inclined to adopt any new theory, or any new mode of treatment that may have been proposed." Next, is the fact that "if the arts of medicine and surgery had never been invented, by far the greater number of those who suffer from bodily illness would have recovered nevertheless"; hence "if any one were to engage in practice, giving his patients nothing but distilled water, and enjoining a careful diet and a prudent method of life otherwise, a certain number of his patients would perish for want of further help, but more would recover;[1] and homœopathic globules are, I doubt not, quite as good as distilled water." Thirdly, comes the fact that a great number of persons, especially in the upper classes, "who have plenty of money, combined with a great lack of employment, contrive, to an astonishing extent, to imagine diseases for themselves," or suffer from uneasy feelings due to want of exercise, irregularity of diet, or worry of mind, to which constant attention "will give a reality which they would not have had otherwise; and such feelings will disappear as well under the use of globules as they would

[1] See Appendix K, Brodie on the *Vis Medicatrix Naturæ*.

under any other mode of treatment or under no treatment at all." And to these causes he adds the errors of diagnosis and treatment, which must occur to some extent in regular practice so long as it is carried on by fallible men. He admits that in many cases homœopathy may be harmless, but points out that where active treatment and accurate diagnosis are necessary the patient fares ill under a system which really involves a negation of all medical treatment and in the hands of persons "who very probably never studied disease at all."

Finally, in reference to homœopathy, as to all other forms of quackery, he urges that "the medical profession must be content to let the thing take its course ; they will best consult their own dignity and the good of the public by saying as little about it as possible. There was a time when many of the medical profession held the opinion† that not only homœopathy, but all other kinds of quackery, ought to be put down by the strong hand of the law. I imagine that there are very few who hold that opinion now. The fact is that the thing is impossible ; and even if it were possible—as it is plain that the profession cannot do all that is wanted of them by curing all kinds of diseases and making men immortal—such an interference with the liberty of individuals to consult whom they please would be absurd and wrong."

It is well, I think, to put on record these opinions on the subject of quackery, deliberately expressed at the close of a long life by one of the most sagacious and one of the most successful practitioners of legitimate medicine.

There is always a tendency on the part of medical men who see quacks flourishing, not only in spite of their ignorance, but even partly because of it, to cry out for protection against such impostors, and to allege the example of the profession of the law, in which no one is permitted to practice who has not been properly educated and regularly admitted. But the analogy is entirely fallacious. The object of preventing sham lawyers from practising is to protect the public from fraud, not to protect the lawyers. Courts of justice and their officers—the solicitors and barristers—would obtain a vast increase of business if every swindler were allowed to pass himself off as a lawyer and plunge his victim's affairs into confusion. The more correct analogy is with the clerical profession: To prevent a man or woman from seeking advice for bodily ailments from a friend or stranger, however unqualified to give it, would be as tyrannical as to forbid such a friend from giving advice in spiritual troubles. But, fortunately, it is utterly impossible. As every one may invent his own religion, and constitute himself and his friends its priests, if he chooses ; so every one is, and ought to be, at liberty to construct his own theory of medicine (even if it is as absurd as homœopathy) and persuade people to adopt it and to employ him, if they like, provided only that he does not represent himself as being legally qualified unless he is so. The persons who, being legally qualified, practice homœopathy, or who will do whichever their patients wish (like the doctor in " Bombastes Furioso," "who suits his physic to his patient's taste "), must be left to their own consciences, such as they are, and to the contempt of those who understand their position. Though the existence of such persons may tend to keep up the delusion, it cannot do much substantial harm to the public. ✗

It was in 1843 that the remarkable case of Mr. Brunel occurred. This gentleman (the engineer of the Great Western Railway, and designer of the monster steamship *Great Eastern*) was unlucky enough to inhale a half-sovereign with which he was playing conjuring tricks to amuse some children. Brodie gives in the " Med. Chir. Trans.," vol. xxvi., a clear and concise history of the various steps taken to extract this small, slippery, heavy body from its position deep in the chest, in or near the right lung. These measures were ultimately crowned with success. First, the patient was put into a revolving frame, and his whole body inverted, head downwards. This caused the coin to drop into the larynx ; but the vocal cords closed on it spasmodically, and the spasms were nearly fatal. Next a large opening was made in the windpipe (tracheotomy), and attempts were made to catch the coin with forceps, introduced through the wound ; but this was found impracticable, and it was seen that fatal mischief might easily be done in the attempt. But afterwards, on repeating the inversion of the body, the coin dropped quietly into the patient's mouth, for the opening into the trachea, below the larynx, obviated the spasms which had before nearly proved fatal. It is said that the machine for the inversion was designed by the patient himself.

In 1849 a strange scandal occurred among the staff of St. George's Hospital, which must, I think, be referred to in Brodie's Life, as he was to some extent mixed up in it, and was blamed as having unfairly advocated a baseless charge against one of his colleagues. The singular history of this scandalous affair was first published in the *St. George's Hospital Gazette* (vol. i. p. 19) by Dr. Howship Dickinson, and I give his account of it. Drs. "Chambers and Seymour had been colleagues as physicians to the hospital, but were not upon the best of terms. . . . At the time of which I speak Chambers had left the hospital ; Seymour still held office. Certain anonymous letters of an injurious character were received by Chambers, and attributed to Seymour, in whose handwriting they apparently were. These were referred to Seymour's colleagues, and by them to experts in handwriting (the most inexpert, as it has always seemed to me, of all experts), with a general concurrence in Seymour's guilt. Dr. Wilson alone demurred. . . . Seymour was charged ; he refused to discuss the matter, and used language of a violence which was thought to be evidence against him. The letters were of a kind to excite indignation, and Seymour's reputation received an injury from which it never recovered. Many years afterwards, when Chambers had been gathered to his fathers, and Seymour was broken down with age and infirmity, a lady, who was dying on the shore of the Mediterranean, sent an earnest request to Dr. Thomas

King Chambers (Dr. Chambers's nephew) to come and see her, as she had something to reveal before she died. The revelation was to the effect that this lady, together with another lady, her coeval, then both young, had invented and carried out the plot without accessory or accomplice. The ladies in question were both entirely unconnected with Dr. Seymour. What was the motive of the conspiracy I will not discuss. If to enrage Chambers, or ruin Seymour, both objects were attained. The main purpose, presumably, had more reference to Chambers than to Seymour. Upon his return to England, charged with this confession, Dr. T. K. Chambers at once carried it to Dr. Wilson and then to Dr. Seymour, proposing to Dr. Seymour to make it known in any manner he wished. To Dr. Seymour it came too late ; he desired to hear no more of the subject, which was accordingly left at rest."

I will imitate Dr. Dickinson's reticence in not discussing the motive of this extraordinary development of female spite, nor the nature of the anonymous letters which these ladies concocted.

In this most unhappy affair Brodie and Dr. Nairne acted for Dr. Chambers, who was ill, while Dr. Seymour put himself into the hands of a friend occupying a high position at the Bar, and some correspondence which passed between the parties in 1849 was printed for private circulation, and afterwards published *in extenso* in the *Lancet* for August 18, 1849. The intervention of the legal gentleman seems to me rather to "embroil the fray," which otherwise is conducted in a manner not discreditable to gentlemen. Dr. Seymour, on being shown the anonymous letters on April 3, 1849, declared on his honour before Brodie and Nairne that he had had nothing to do with them. They accepted this declaration as perfectly satisfactory to them, and on the instance of Dr. Seymour's legal friend procured a letter from Dr. Chambers to the same effect. But Brodie and Nairne would not admit that the suspicion had been an absurd one, nor would they apologise for having entertained it. And this was, no doubt, the gravamen of the accusation, because as Dr. Dickinson says, "Seymour's reputation received an injury from which it never recovered." Every one believed that though the accusation against Dr. Seymour was not proved, "there was a good deal in it." No doubt in this, as in all such affairs, the impartial spectator would find that all the parties were more or less wrong. Seymour ought not to have been above discussing the matter calmly. The medical staff, instead of relying on the opinion of an "expert," ought to have done at once what was done afterwards, *i.e.*, appealed to Dr. Seymour's honour. Chambers ought not to have been so prone to entertain the suspicion. His friends, when they withdrew the accusation, ought to have done so more frankly. Seymour's legal friend ought to have managed the matter in a less legal spirit. But the suspicion was really not an absurd one, if I may trust the account of those who were concerned in investigating the matter; the letters had been very cleverly concocted, the conspirators being well acquainted with Seymour's epistolary style, and having imitated it, as well as his writing, with diabolical dexterity, and no doubt Seymour's conduct did much to confirm his colleague's suspicions ; more especially some letters from him to a lady, a friend and patient of Dr. Chambers, in which that gentleman seems to have been spoken of disrespectfully. The matter was treated of in leading articles by the *Lancet*, May 12th, and August 18, 1849, and some of the circumstances attending it were referred to the College of Physicians, who, however, avoided the public scandal which the investigation would have caused.

In the year 1849 Sir Benjamin Brodie became President of the Western Medical and Surgical Society of London, then newly founded among men practising medicine in the West of London, but which has now, as most local societies do, finished its work and given place to the more permanent associations.[1] He has left us (vol. i. p. 539) an Address which he delivered as President in 1850, which certainly deserved preservation and a wider audience than the one to which it was originally spoken, for it is really a noble speech, setting forth in a very few and simple words the judgment which this great surgeon, now at the head of the whole medical world, had formed of the worth of the profession itself, and of the spirit in which its

---

[1] The Society was founded in 1845. It was dissolved in 1871, and the books which belonged to it were handed over to the Library of St. George's Hospital.

practice ought to be pursued. On both of these great topics his utterances are most elevated and most elevating. He looks at the profession of medicine not as a trade, but as a noble pursuit, which, in spite of the ceaseless labour, the endless anxieties and the crushing responsibilities which it entails,[1] is able to give abundant compensation in elevation of mind, freedom from prejudice, and the sense of having so lived as to have been serviceable to one's fellow-man.

His views on the spirit in which this high calling should be followed are equally noble. In the first place he urges on his fellow-members how much we gain by regarding " our competitors as our friends, with whom we are on such a footing that we mutually make allowance for each other's feelings, and are on all occasions ready to do justice to each other's good qualities, whether of the head or heart " (p. 539). And he goes on to say that this same charitable wisdom should be extended to all our fellow-men. " After a long experience of the world I have come to the conclusion that the true way of dealing with mankind is, as a general rule, to trust to their good qualities rather than to the controlling of

---

[1] Thus in speaking of the branch of it which he had himself pursued, he says in words the full force of which can only be felt by one who has stood in the same position, and who can recollect the early days of his hospital practice, " I am confident that there is no situation more trying to him who holds it than that of the young hospital surgeon, exposed (as he very probably is) to the remarks and criticisms of the public ; nor any in which there is less repose for the mind, or greater reason to feel anxiety as to the future, than that of an individual whose practice is confined to surgery."

their bad ones. . . .[1] To suspect another of being influenced by unworthy motives is to degrade him in his own estimation, and there is nothing which a proud and independent spirit will find it so difficult to forgive ; as, on the other hand, there are few persons who will not feel some sort of gratitude for having the most favourable construction put on their conduct, even when their conscience tells them that it is more than they really merit " (p. 540). And even the annoyances to which medical men are so peculiarly exposed from the hasty judgments, the perverseness and caprices of those among whom they practice, are to be looked upon, according to this truly wise man of the world, in the same liberal and indulgent spirit. "We have to a great extent," he says, "the power of relieving pain[2] and preserving life, but our power is limited ; on the other hand, there is no limit to the desire of obtaining relief, and the anxiety to live may still linger in those who are on the point of death. Under these circumstances, it seems almost a matter of course that those to whom we can render no further aid, and whose minds are probably weakened by previous illness, should be easily induced to seek for aid elsewhere, and be ready to listen to any promises of men, however vain and absurd, or even dishonest, those promises may be. Taking all things into consideration, it appears to me to be a question whether

---

[1] See Appendix L, Brodie on self-respect and self-help.

[2] On the tablet in Betchworth Church are the following words : " By his surgical skill he alleviated the sufferings of his own generation and conferred lasting benefits on mankind."

there is not, on the whole, more cause for wonder in the patience of the many than in the impatience of the few ; and whether the gratitude of those who over-estimate our services does not even more than compensate for the neglect of those who withhold from us the credit which we really deserve."

There are those who can see in medical practice (to use the vigorous words of Dr. Johnson) only "melancholy attendance on misery, mean submission to peevishness, and continual interruption of rest and pleasure," [1] but these are usually men who have failed of success, and for this failure they have usually to thank themselves in great measure, as Brodie had to thank himself in great measure—his keen intellect and his untiring energy—for his great success. But one cannot doubt that his success was also largely due to that elevation of mind which rendered jealousy a feeling to which he was a stranger, and to that true knowledge of the world which is dictated by a warm heart and a philanthropic disposition.

In 1850 (June 29) occurred the sad accident which proved fatal to Sir Robert Peel. Sir Robert was riding quietly up Constitution Hill, when he was thrown from his horse and fell heavily, injuring his left shoulder and chest. Sir Benjamin Brodie, Mr. Hodgson, Mr. Cæsar Hawkins, and others were called to attend him, and amongst Brodie's papers is a detailed account of the case. The main interest in it, from a surgical point of view, is to observe how probable it is that if anæsthesia had been as familiar

[1] "Rambler," No. 19.

as it now is, the case might have been treated with success, and so valuable a life have been spared. The clavicle was fractured and comminuted, and there can be little doubt that one of the fragments had wounded either the subclavian or internal jugular vein,[1] producing hæmorrhage which proved gradually fatal. Sir Robert's excessive sensitiveness to pain prevented even any sufficient examination of the injury, far less any attempt to treat it. But if he had been brought under anæsthesia it might have been easy to have put the broken bone in place, or removed it, and if necessary secured the wounded vein. But all this was out of the question at that time. Nothing effectual could be done, and in a little more than three days this great man's life ended. The exact injury was not ascertained, as a post-mortem examination was objected to ; but the account leaves no doubt of the nature of the injury, though the exact position of the wound in the vein remains, of course, uncertain.[2]

Amongst the multifarious activities and the varied studies for which he found time, side by side with his professional labours, we find him in 1853 presiding over the Ethnological Society.

Of him, as much as of any man who ever lived, it might be said that he thought nothing which con-

---

[1] A few years after this event a boy was brought into St. George's Hospital, dead, having been struck on the shoulder by a branch torn off a tree in Hyde Park in a storm. The clavicle had been fractured and a fragment had lacerated the internal jugular vein close to its junction with the subclavian. Mr. Cæsar Hawkins was struck with the similarity of the injury to that which proved fatal to Sir Robert Peel.

[2] See Appendix M for Brodie's account of Sir Robert Peel's case.

cerned humanity alien from his business ; and therefore
he took up with interest, and seems to have followed
to some extent, those most important researches which
anthropologists (as they now style themselves) had
then just begun to make into the development of
the race, of its institutions, its morals, and its religion.
His address on this occasion is found in his collected
works (vol. i. p. 547). There is nothing in it, I
dare say, of any value now, after the investigations
of forty-five years ; but it is written in the same
lucid style and in the same liberal and fearless spirit
which characterise Brodie's other works, and it
concludes with a prediction, which time has abundantly
verified, that the objects of the Society will advance
year by year in reputation and usefulness, and that
the science will be ranked amongst the most important
of the age.

VIII

1854–1862

CLOSING YEARS

"Above all, believe it, the sweetest canticle is 'Nunc dimittis,' when
a man hath obtained worthy ends and expectations."—BACON.

IN the year 1856 occurred the celebrated trial of
William Palmer, a medical man, for the murder
of an associate in horse-racing transactions, named
Cook. This trial profoundly interested the public in
consequence of the singular circumstances under
which the murder was committed, and the great
ingenuity which Palmer had displayed in conveying
the poison to his victim in such a way that it might
seem as if Cook had never received any medicine
whatever from him, and from the neighbouring
chemist only some pills of a perfectly harmless nature

177

which Palmer had prescribed.[1] The trial was not
less interesting to the medical profession from the
new questions in toxicology which it raised, especially
in connection with strychnia-poisoning. And it
showed Brodie in a new light—as a medical witness.
No more perfect model of medical evidence can be
produced than his in this trial, as reported in the
Times for May 19, 1856. It is short, clear, and
decisive, and the reporter adds, "Sir Benjamin Brodie
gave his evidence with great clearness—slowly, audibly,
and distinctly—matters in which other medical men
would do well to emulate so distinguished an example."
We may add that his answers, though most exact from
a medical point of view, are perfectly free from all
pedantry, and quite intelligible to any layman.
The question was twofold. 1. Was the case one of
idiopathic tetanus or of poisoning? 2. Was it
poisoning or epilepsy?—or, as one of the medical
witnesses called by the defence phrased it—"epilepsy
with tetanic complications"? Brodie speaks to the
rarity of idiopathic tetanus as compared with traumatic
(of which there could be no question in this case), to
the different course of the symptoms, which in tetanus
always, or almost always, begin with lockjaw—here
with general convulsions—while in tetanus, as the
symptoms go on, the muscles of the neck and spine
are affected—rarely those of the extremities, and
hardly ever of the hand, as in this case. He testifies
also that ordinary tetanus hardly ever terminates in

[1] An account of this trial is given by Serjeant Ballantine in his
Reminiscences, chap. xvi.

so short a space of time as twelve hours, and never disappears, as in this case, to recur after an interval of twenty-four hours and prove fatal. Finally, he says, the symptoms were not those of apoplexy, nor of epilepsy, nor of any disease known to him.

This evidence was entirely incontrovertible, and had great influence on the verdict—a verdict the justice of which has never been questioned. There can be no doubt that Cook was first made ill with antimony and then killed by strychnine, administered first in an insufficient,[1] and next day in a poisonous dose.

If all medical witnesses would follow Brodie's example, as set in this case, professional testimony would rise in public and in forensic estimation ; we should cease to look on the degrading spectacle of witnesses who seem to be as much retained for one side or the other as the advocates are. They would speak to matters of fact, resting on the sure ground of their own and others' experience, avoiding dubious hypotheses and the wranglings of pretended "science";[2] and, speaking in plain English, without bombast or technicality, they would guide and assist · the Court in forming a just judgment, instead of misleading and confusing it.

---

[1] The insufficiency of the first dose might have been accidental, or it might have been calculated, so as to accustom Cook's friends and attendants to the symptoms which were afterwards to prove fatal ; or it might well be that Palmer was trying to produce death with the smallest possible dose, for there was some evidence of his belief that such a dose would not leave any residue detectable in the dead body.

[2] ἀντιθέσεις τῆς ψευδωνύμου γνώσεως (1 Tim. vi. 20).

On August 15, 1859, another remarkable trial took place, in which Brodie's assistance was invoked in order to prevent a miscarriage of justice. A man named Smethurst, a medical practitioner, was living at Richmond with a lady who passed as his wife.[1] She had some property which she had bequeathed to Smethurst, in her maiden name, knowing that the form of marriage which she had gone through with him was void, because Smethurst's wife was alive—and was indeed cognisant of the whole transaction. The *soi-disant* Mrs. Smethurst became very ill—persistent vomiting being a prominent symptom. She called in a well-known Richmond medical man, now deceased, who, suspecting foul play, got his partner to see her, without telling him anything of the circumstances, and as he conceived the same suspicion they called in a physician who at that time was perhaps the leading man in London consulting practice, again without telling him anything as to the suspicious nature of the case. He at once pronounced to his two consultants the same opinion—viz., that the case was one of irritant poisoning. Yet, strange to say, none of the three took any steps to save the poor woman's life. After her death the body was examined. Traces of antimony and of arsenic were found, and Smethurst was put on his trial. After a prolonged investigation he was found guilty and sentenced to death. But great dissatisfaction was felt with the verdict, for the very important fact

---

[1] This trial also is related by Serjeant Ballantine in chap. xxvi. of the work above referred to.

that the woman was pregnant had not been ascertained during life, and was only revealed by a post-mortem examination ; and the accuracy of the chemical tests employed to prove the presence of arsenic was seriously questioned by competent persons. The defence, therefore, was set up that the dysentery which caused death was a complication of pregnancy, not caused by irritant poison ; and the case of the celebrated Charlotte Brontë, who was said to have died from this cause, was used with much effect on the public, who had been deeply touched by the recent death of this gifted writer, also in an early stage of pregnancy. The Home Secretary of the day, Sir G. C. Lewis, granted a reprieve, and sent the papers to Brodie for his opinion. This opinion coincided with that which he had himself formed—viz., that though the facts were full of suspicion against Smethurst, they were not absolutely conclusive of his guilt. Smethurst therefore received a free pardon for the murder, but was tried for the bigamy and received the severe sentence of a year's hard labour, on his release from which he brought a suit into the Probate Court, and recovered the property devised to him by the will of the unfortunate woman whom he had first ruined and then very likely murdered.

The case was noteworthy in many respects. It is mentioned here as a proof of the leading position which Sir Benjamin Brodie then occupied in the eyes of the public, and of the confidence with which his opinion was accepted, even in a matter so remote as this from surgery. But of course its importance to the medical profession and to the public was due to far different causes. Medical men asked themselves whether those who attended this unfortunate lady in her life-time had acted rightly. Her medical attendants had the strongest reason for suspecting murder, and they had a conviction that the patient was being murdered before their eyes. Yet they did nothing to prevent it, and the patient died, in all probability from the cause which they suspected. No doubt the fact that the putative husband, and suspected murderer, was a medical man rendered action in this case more difficult, yet it has always appeared to me that they might have declined to be further responsible for the case unless they were allowed to provide a night and a day nurse, through whose hands alone all food and medicine was to pass to the patient. The husband could hardly have ventured to refuse this.[1] Nor need it have alarmed the patient. The case at any rate raised a question regarding the duties of medical attendants which, as far as I know, is still unsettled.

Even more important is the problem of the revision of sentences, involved in many other cases as well, but which was, perhaps, even more forcibly illustrated in Smethurst's than in any of the *causes célèbres* which have since raised the same point. The Home Secretary was pelted with petitions got up by ladies who went from house to house canvassing for signatures, and obtaining them from people who knew no

[1] In a letter which Smethurst had the hardihood to write to the *Lancet* he said that he would have willingly assented to such an arrangement.

more of the principles of medical jurisprudence or the phenomena of poisoning than they knew of Hebrew, and the case was retried in the newspapers with the obvious intention of appealing to the fears of the Home Secretary, for what his sense of justice might not have induced him to concede.

In 1857 Brodie, who had taken an active part in the inauguration of the National Association for the Promotion of Social Science, officiated at its first meeting as President of the Section of Social Economy. His address on this occasion is preserved in his collected works (vol. i. p. 553), and it contains at any rate one portion which seems to me of peculiar interest, as showing how strongly he then felt the need of organisation in our metropolitan charities. He first refers to the various ways in which public charity may do harm, if ill-devised or ill-administered. First he speaks of the Poor Law, which, although "a necessary part of our system," produced most evil effects when administered as it was formerly in an agricultural population, where he had himself seen sturdy labourers going "on a Saturday evening to the house of the overseer to claim as a right an addition to their too low wages, in proportion, not to their industry and skill and their amount of labour, but in proportion to the number of their families." So that improvident marriages were directly encouraged. And even at the date of his address, and in London, he points out that working men were encouraged to spend their wages on drink by the knowledge that their wives and children could never starve, as whatever happens the parish must maintain them. Then he turns to the numerous public charities, and shows how large is the proportion of such as attract idle and undeserving people to neighbourhoods "where there is a great deal of money given away"; what harm in this way is done by almshouses; how much money is spent with no public advantage on the machinery of charity; what drawbacks attend the system of "voting charities"; and, finally, how this extension of public charity tends to discourage private charity, which, "if carefully distributed, is a much better thing." "Any one," he concludes, "who would be at the pains of doing it, might collect much valuable information on these subjects, which would be useful in directing the liberality of the public. It might be shown under what circumstances the operation of such charities is beneficial; under what other circumstances it is injurious; and it might also be shown how the money contributed may be applied to the purposes for which it was given, and not be wasted, as it often is, by expenditure in other ways."

It has long been my great pleasure and, as I esteem it, my great honour to work in conjunction with the Society which so zealously and so ably seeks to compass these objects, and I rejoice to think that the Charity Organisation Society can plead for its general aims and the motives of its institution not only the great example of Chalmers, but also the enlightened precepts of Brodie.

The Medical Act, passed in the year 1858, created the General Medical Council, and of this Council Sir

Benjamin Brodie was chosen President, as was only natural, for he was at that time indisputably the most distinguished and the most authoritative member of the profession. He held the post until June 1860, when he resigned, probably because he felt the approach of the weakness of vision which soon became more apparent, and which put a stop to all activity.

The chief functions of this Council concern the general relations of the medical profession to the public, and the regulation of medical education. On both subjects Sir Benjamin's ideas were enlightened and liberal. We have already seen (p. 165) how ardently he deprecated the impracticable and degrading proposal to fence in the practice of medicine by legal prohibition of quackery, and how vigorously he insisted that the profession should " depend solely on the skill, character and conduct of its members," and not " be bolstered up by an Act of Parliament." Still, it is necessary for the protection both of the public and of the practitioner that the latter should have some testimonial, in the nature of a diploma, of his having completed a proper course of education, and passed a proper examination. Without some public supervision a host of fraudulent institutions would spring up which would sell their diplomas to persons who had neither been properly educated nor seriously examined. And even some institutions of more respectable origin might (to judge from experience) be tempted to confer titles in exchange for fees, rather than as a testamur of merit.

It is necessary also to have some power of censor-
ship by which persons regularly qualified may be
removed from the ranks of the profession if guilty of
criminal or disgraceful conduct.   Hence the system
of registration which the Act introduced, together
with the powers conferred on the Council to strike a
name off the register on cause shown—subject, of
course, to the right of a court of law to reverse their
decision, if erroneous.   No one is prevented from
employing a quack if he likes to do so, no quack is
punished for practising as such, though he is punishable
for manslaughter if he should commit it, and for fraud
if he should falsely represent himself as a registered
practitioner.   This was precisely the liberal and
sensible plan which Brodie had always advocated.

On the subject of medical education his views were
equally enlightened.   We have seen above how much
thought and care he had given to the subject, how he
had worked at it at the College of Surgeons, and how
successfully he had laboured to introduce a higher
form of examination at the College as the qualification
for a higher order of members.   But so acute a mind
as his must have seen that there can be no finality in
the mode of education and examination applicable to
a profession so constantly progressive as that of medicine is ; and that some authority is needed to
introduce or sanction the alterations in medical
education and examination rendered necessary by the
changing conditions of medical theory and practice.
In this country such an authority cannot be what is
vaguely called "the Government," by which is meant

the anonymous advisers of one of the Ministers. It must be some body of properly qualified men meeting and deliberating in public. The General Medical Council may not, up to this time, have fulfilled all the expectations of its authors, but its central idea is indisputably good and liberal, and there is much reason to hope and to believe that its progress will be more rapid in the future than it has been since Brodie's day. He was succeeded in his office of president of the Medical Council by Mr. Green, the illustrious surgeon who is now best known as the friend, the pupil, and the literary executor of Coleridge.

The appointment to the presidency of the General Medical Council and that to the chair of the Royal Society were almost simultaneous. A writer in the *Lancet* of November 27, 1858, speaks thus: "The honour of election to the office of President of the General Medical Council, which on Tuesday night befell Sir B. Brodie, is the highest which the profession has in its gift. On Monday next Sir Benjamin Brodie will be elected President of the Royal Society. It is a rare fortune which crowds distinctions so singular within the space of a few days. It is perhaps as unusual that they should be bestowed by common consent and amid general plaudits. . . . Now is the time for the Prime Minister of England to confer a peerage upon a distinguished member of our profession. Such a man as Sir B. Brodie would add lustre to the House of Lords. . . . We have reason to believe that our wishes in this respect will be fulfilled, as it is confidently stated that Sir Benjamin Brodie is to be raised to the peerage with the title of Baron Betch-worth of Betchworth, Surrey. Why not Lord Brodie ? "

Confidently, however, as the statement might be made, it received prompt official contradiction when copied, as it soon was, into the *Times*.

I have not been able to discover exactly what amount of foundation there is for the rumour, which has prevailed ever since those days, that a peerage for Sir Benjamin Brodie was, if not actually offered, yet in contemplation, and that the matter was mentioned to Brodie. At any rate the rumour was so public that it reached the ear of the person concerned. An obviously well-informed writer in the *British Medical Journal*, in reviewing Brodie's life, says, "He considered the Presidency of the Royal Society the greatest honour that had been conferred upon him; and, as he himself observed when a peerage was spoken of, he prized it above any peerage." [1]

Lord Derby was Prime Minister in 1858, when this matter was discussed in the *Lancet*. It was in the year 1856 that Lord Palmerston attempted to form a class of life-peers, and had a patent of life peerage issued to Baron Parke, of the Exchequer, in order to test the powers of the Crown to confer such a dignity. The attempt was defeated by the House of Lords, acting under Lord Derby's leadership. Had it succeeded, there seems hardly room for doubt

[1] See Mr. Charles Hawkins's "In Memoriam," vol. i, p. xvii. It is very clear from a letter written about this time that a peerage was not at all an honour which Brodie desired.

that Brodie would have been nominated a life-peer.
And many professional men regretted the failure of
Lord Palmerston's scheme, considering the many
advantages which it seemed to hold out to men
of various professions, especially to medical men.
Churchmen have for many ages enjoyed life peerages
as bishops. Lawyers now have them, as Lords of
Appeal, and with much advantage to Parliament in
both cases. Men of letters have in two celebrated
cases—Macaulay and Tennyson—been able to accept
a hereditary title; but one of these was a bachelor.
Now medical men are very rarely rich enough to bear
the weight of a hereditary peerage, nor can they, if of
the first rank, spare the time to enter the House of
Commons. Yet there are many public questions on
which the counsels of medical men are of the first
importance; and it is obvious that such counsels are
of far more public worth if given by a member of the
legislature speaking publicly, and with the weight of a
well-earned authority, than if given in private to a
Minister by some unknown person. It seems to me
almost equally obvious how great advantages would
accrue to the House of Lords and to the public if that
august assembly were reinforced by the presence of
men who are eminent in the various arts of peace and
war, but who are not able or perhaps even willing to
transmit their honours to their posterity. For it is
not every one who would like to face the chance that
his title may be borne hereafter by some one whose
defects may be as notorious as its first holder's excellences were distinguished.

BRODIE

The Presidency of the Royal Society, in which he succeeded Lord Wrottesley was, as we have seen, an honour which he valued much more than a Peerage ; and it was an eminence to which no surgeon had previously risen. The only physicians who have been thought worthy of this great distinction were Sir Hans Sloane and Sir John Pringle, besides Wollaston, who, however, threw up both the Presidency and the profession, in disgust, when he was rejected as a candidate for the office of Physician to St. George's Hospital. The great man who now fills the chair of the Royal Society is the second surgeon who has held that office ; and the one who has probably succeeded more than any other person who has yet lived, in applying science directly to the saving of human life, as Brodie may be said to have been the one who succeeded more than all his predecessors in connecting the pursuit of surgery with the cultivation of science in general. It was John Hunter indeed who first established the connection between surgery and the science of physiology, and who thus became, as his monument in Westminster Abbey justly styles him, "The Founder of Scientific Surgery" ; but it was Brodie's peculiar glory, his main title to posthumous fame, to have carried this connection further and to have shown how much the practice of surgery may gain from the possession by its professor of a competent acquaintance with physical science in general ; and how much he may thereby raise the whole profession in the estimation of the public. I do not intend to represent that Sir Benjamin Brodie was a profound

man of science, as his former colleague Dr. Thomas
Young, no doubt was ; but he was well versed in all
the science of his day. He had in his younger days
studied physiology deeply, and had done much by his
personal labours for its advancement ; he was also
well grounded in mental science, and was one of the
pioneers of what is called Social Science (though
whether it deserves the title I leave to others to
judge) ; and above and beyond all these claims to
preside over the Royal Society is the fact that he
brought scientific knowledge and the scientific spirit
to bear on his surgical teaching and practice. Dr.
Young was one of the greatest physical philosophers
of his age ; one of the most universal geniuses of any
age ; and he was also a physician, and apparently a
good one. But his career as a physician was in no
respect affected by his philosophic pursuits, any more
than if the Dr. Young who was physician to St.
George's Hospital, had been a different man from the
one who deciphered the hieroglyphics of Egypt and
promulgated the undulatory theory of light.

The addresses which Brodie delivered at the Royal
Society—four in number, viz., on taking the chair in
December, 1858, and at the annual meetings of the
three following years, are preserved in the first volume
of his collected works. They show how faithfully he
retained, at this late period of his life, the tastes and
habits which had led him to success in youth.
" The first step," he says, " in all physical investigations, even in those which admit of the application of
mathematical reasoning, and the deductive method

afterwards, is the observation of natural phenomena, and the smallest error in such observation in the beginning is sufficient to vitiate the whole investigation afterwards. The necessity of strict and minute observation, then, is the first thing which the student of the physical sciences has to learn, and it is easy to see with what great advantage the habit thus acquired may be carried into everything else afterwards." Do we not recognise in these words a reminiscence of the old times when he learned from Jeffreys the importance of taking notes (see p. 37) and of the long course of successful practice to which that habit of close and accurate observation had been the worthy introduction ?

These addresses contain also much that is interesting in other ways. I would refer to his pregnant remark that "physical observations more than anything else help to teach us the actual value and the right use of the imagination—of that wonderful faculty which, . . . properly restrained by experience and reflexion, becomes the noblest attribute of man, the source of poetic genius ; the instrument of discovery in science, without the aid of which Newton would never have invented fluxions, nor Davy have decomposed the earths and alkaloids, nor Columbus have found another continent beyond the Atlantic Ocean ;" and the striking examples which he gives of the importance of the imagination in matters of science, drawn from Oersted's discovery of the identity of electricity and magnetism, and Stahl's refuted doctrine of "phlogiston."

Another interesting passage is that in which he

refers to Hume's suggestion that the same methods of inquiry which had been applied with so great advantage to astronomy and other physical sciences, might also be applicable " to those other sciences which have for their object the mental power and economy." In this connection Brodie's long application to mental science and the zeal with which he had pursued the study of such authors as Locke, Berkeley, Reid, and Dugald Stewart stood him in good stead in showing him how much modern British authors (for of the Germans he confesses his ignorance) have done to realise and even anticipate Hume's wishes, and how the lucidity of the Scotch school of metaphysicians, as compared with the dreamy speculations of earlier days, is due " to their having in their mode of inquiry followed the example which had been set them in the study of the physical sciences."

The last of these discourses was pronounced on November 30, 1861, and derives a pathetic interest from the circumstances under which he had accepted re-nomination to the Presidency the previous year. He had then been uncertain whether the condition of his eyesight would permit him to discharge the onerous duties of the Presidency, but in hopes that the operation which was then contemplated would preserve for him useful vision in one eye, he had yielded to the unanimous wishes of the Council by consenting to occupy the chair for another year. Those hopes had been frustated. He had been unable during a whole session to take part in the meetings; and he now resigns, in a few dignified and well-chosen words, into the hands of the Society, the great trust which he had so faithfully discharged. But this short address shows that his interest in science had not been diminished by age and blindness, by domestic bereavement and the near prospect of death. It shows how he still felt not only "the love of knowledge," but also "that desire of honourable distinction, *that last infirmity of noble minds*," which he here speaks of as the all-sufficient inducements to the cultivation of science. It is refreshing to find in this last communication of Brodie to the scientific world the same manly spirit of independence which he displayed in all the other phases of his varied career. "I cannot join," he says, "with those who complain that the interest of science has been neglected by the Government. The Fellows of the Royal Society have never wished to forfeit their independence by claiming, in their capacity of Fellows, any personal benefit for themselves," and he shows how far it would be from a benefit to the Society or to science if the Royal Society, with its unrestricted fellowship and unfettered freedom, could be transformed into the likeness of a Continental Academy, limited in number, and with a stipend from the public treasury. The closing observations on the presentation of medals to Prof. Agassiz for his researches in natural history, in palæontology, and in the glacial theory ; to Dr. Carpenter for his researches on the Foraminifera and other investigations in natural history ; and to Prof. Sylvester for his mathematical researches, prove how wide was his sympathy with the most various branches of science, and how well he had contrived to keep abreast of them, in spite of his heavy afflictions.

Towards the end of Brodie's life, the great spread of specialism in medicine, and the establishment of many large institutions for the treatment of special diseases, began to operate unfavourably on the general hospitals, and attracted the attention of the profession. A protest was signed by five hundred medical men, and published in the public papers, against the establishment of special hospitals as injurious to the general hospitals, as tending to withdraw the diseases in question from the observation of the medical students, and as a source of unnecessary expense to the public, by founding separate establishments for the treatment of affections which could be as well or better treated at institutions already founded and much in want of funds.

So strongly did Brodie feel on this subject that he not only signed the protest, but accompanied his signature with a letter, setting forth these objections to special hospitals, which was published in the *British Medical Journal* for July 28, 1860, and other papers, and is included in his collected works, vol. i. p. 658.

On August 31, 1860, Brodie published a letter in the *Times* on the use and abuse of tobacco, marked by the moderation and good sense which characterise all his writing. It is hardly necessary to say that he does not imitate the extravagance of those fanatics who see in the balmy weed which " from east to west cheers the tar's labours and the Turkman's rest," a " gorging fiend," or a deadly poison. He quite admits

that "if tobacco-smokers would limit themselves to
the occasional indulgence of their appetite they would
do little harm either to themselves or others," while
he draws a gloomy picture of the possible consequences
of excessive smoking, both to the individual and his
offspring, a picture which the ampler experience of
the present day—due to the great extension of the
habit—would, I think, confirm in some cases, though
these may be exceptional. But Brodie's personal
experience of the habit was, I believe, a negative
quantity. When he was young, "tobacco-smoking,"
as he says, "was almost wholly confined to what are
commonly called the lower grades of society. It was
only every now and then that any one who wished
to be considered a gentleman was addicted to it."
How different things are now, when not only almost
every one who wishes to be considered a gentleman,
but many who wish to be considered as ladies are
addicted to the habit!

The close of Brodie's long and prosperous life was
not exempt from the ordinary calamities which sit at
the "sad threshold of old age." [1] His wife, to whom
he had been so long and so tenderly attached, died in
July, 1861. We have no record of the grief of the
old man now left alone, but we know what a happy
life he had led with her for forty-five years, and how
ardent his affections were, and so can well conceive
what he must have felt. He had been then, for about
a year, suffering from progressive loss of vision. It
was in July, 1860, that he was obliged to consult an

---

[1] ὀλόῳ ἐπὶ γήραος οὐδῷ. Il. xxiv., 487.

oculist, and " he submitted to iridectomy on both eyes, afterwards to extraction of a cataract, and finally to an operation for artificial pupil." [1] But all was in vain, nor in fact had his skilful friend Sir William Bowman, who had charge of the case, given any great hope of success ; though in the then condition of ophthalmic surgery it was doubtless right to try the effect of operation. He thus remained practically blind, but he was still in good health, and his mind was still as active as ever. His last public appearance was at a meeting of the Royal Medical and Chirurgical Society on December 31, 1861, soon after the death of the Prince Consort, to vote an address of condolence to the Queen, when he moved the adoption of the address in a speech of high eulogy on the Prince's acquirements and character. [2]

It was in April that he returned to Broome Park, and there he " was seized with severe lumbago followed by protracted fever."

A further complication soon followed. It seems that nearly thirty years previously he had suffered from dislocation of the right shoulder. [3] I am not aware

[1] Ch. Hawkins, "In Memoriam," Works, I. xxiv.

[2] The *Lancet*, January 4, 1862, in reporting the meeting says : "The venerable surgeon, though bearing marks of his advanced age, is still vigorous in mind and speech. The manner of his address was not unworthy of his best days." They add, "It will be gratifying to our readers to learn that the sight of one of the eyes of Sir Benjamin is so much improved as to enable him to write a letter, though he is not able to read for any length of time. His sight, however, is gradually increasing in power."

[3] We read as follows in the *Lancet*, 1862, vol. ii. p. 456 : " Mr. White Cooper tells us that about 1834, while staying at an hotel in the Isle of Wight, he saw a carriage drive up from which was lifted out a

that he ever made any complaint of the part, after the dislocation had been reduced; but it was in this same joint that in July he began to complain of pain, accompanied by much prostration; and this was succeeded in September by the appearance of a tumour, doubtless of a malignant nature, in the neighbourhood of the shoulder. He now sank rapidly, and died on Oct. 21, 1862, retaining perfect consciousness to within a few hours of his death, in the eightieth year of his age.

In the winter of 1861–2 he availed himself of the services of Dr. Reginald Thompson (brother-in-law to the second Sir Benjamin Brodie), who used to spend an hour or two in the afternoon at the house in Portland Place, where Brodie was then residing, in reading over to him his old notes of cases, preserved in several MS. volumes still in the possession of the present Sir Benjamin Brodie, and taking down his observations on them. These are preserved in the third volume of his collected works; and they remain to show how vigorous his intellect still was, and how keen was still

gentleman, covered with mud, and evidently in some pain, who was no other than Sir B. Brodie. He had been thrown from a pony, and was suffering from dislocation of the shoulder. Mr. Bloxam, a well-known practitioner of that day and place, came in, and Mr. White Cooper and Mr. Bloxam together reduced the dislocation. Sir Benjamin said that he used to think lightly of dislocation of the shoulder, but he never should do so again. It was in this joint that fatal disease afterwards showed itself." I may just notice that Mr. Bloxam's name occurs in an old note-book in which Brodie has preserved short notices of cases in his private practice which struck him as interesting. In March, 1844, Mr. Bloxam consulted Sir Benjamin in consequence of having temporarily lost the power of moving the muscles of one side of his face from having been close to a cannon when it was fired. The accident was a curious one; but it seems not to have entailed any permanent consequences.

his interest in the profession to which his life had been devoted.

Dr. R. Thompson has been kind enough to give me some interesting reminiscences of these last days of a great career. Sir Benjamin was never (as long as he saw him) actually blind, but could see his way about the room, and even write a few words, though not very legibly. His physical powers were much enfeebled, and it was sad to see how sorely he felt that his life was ended and his occupation gone. Still he never complained, but bore his troubles with resignation and dignity. The last words which Dr. Thompson heard him say were, " After all, God is very good." He suffered at that time no pain, and his mind was sound and active. He was still interested in all the various pursuits which had filled his life, and was remarkable for his gentleness and kindness to his juniors. He was a man of sincerely religious feelings and principles, but did not speak of such matters much ; and naturally not to a man so much his junior.

In April, 1862, he left for Broome Park ; and it was not till after this time that the painful disease showed itself which seems to have been the direct cause of his death, though he suffered from other troubles also, which obliged him to have recourse to the skilful aid of his friend Mr. Cutler. It is to this closing period of his life that Sir Henry Acland refers in his biographical sketch first published in the Proceedings of the Royal Society. " A fortnight before his death he once more talked to the same person of the mysterious link between our consciousness and our visible material

organisation, descanting with keen interest on the
relations between mind and body, and the mutual
reactions of one on the other. As he then lay on his
sofa, almost for the last time, in great pain, having
scarce for many months seen the outer world which
had been so much to him, and to which he had been
so much, he spoke freely of our ignorance as to many
things which it would be a joy to know—of the existence of evil—of the too little attention which philosophers had paid to the terrible nature of physical pain—
of the future state. So gathering up the teachings of
his useful life, and still, as ever, looking forward, he
waited its close. Not many days after this he breathed
his last . . . in possession of the full calm power of his
disciplined mind to within a few hours of his death," [1]
which took place on Oct. 21. In a letter of which I
have been permitted to make use, his son says : " He
passed away very, very gently, like a little child sinking
to sleep," after "a long and weary struggle—but I hope
that he has suffered nothing."

[1] *Op. cit.*, pp. 29, 30.

IX

BRODIE'S PSYCHOLOGY

"At the time of his death he left his system still incomplete ; or he
may be more truly said to have had no system, but to have lived in the
successive stages or moments of metaphysical thought which presented
themselves from time to time."—JOWETT on Plato. *Introduction to the
Philebus.*

SIR BENJAMIN BRODIE was far indeed
from confining himself to his own profession.
We have seen how from his earliest years he addicted
himself to the study of noble literature, how through
the whole of his busy career as a surgeon he found
time for the scientific study of physiology and its
experimental investigation, how both in his youth
and manhood he cultivated the society of the leaders

in the various schools of science and managed to keep
abreast of the progress of that busy era, not only in
physiology but in most branches of science. It is not
surprising, therefore, to find him stepping out of his
own career and appearing as an author on a very difficult metaphysical subject, viz., psychology. His short
work on this science was published in two parts, of
which the first appeared anonymously in 1854. It
attracted a good deal of attention, and a second edition
was called for "in 1855, a third in 1856, and a fourth
in 1862, just previous to the author's death, in which
year also the second part was published." [1] But,
though it was at first issued without the author's
name, there could have been no real intention of
concealing the authorship; for, besides that it is
written in Brodie's well-marked style, a passage is
repeated in the First Dialogue almost word for word
from the Introductory Discourse at St. George's,
1843.[2]

The work in not intended as a formal treatise on
the entire science. It is correctly described by its
title "Psychological Inquiries," and its object is, not,
like Mr. H. Spencer's ponderous treatise, to form part
of a complete System of Philosophy, but merely to
stimulate his readers to a study then much neglected,
and more especially (as he says in the Preface to Part
II.) to realise the two following objects—*first*, "to show
that the solution of the complicated problem relating

---

[1] Charles Hawkins, vol. i. p. 118.

[2] See Appendix N, About an unconscious Principle of order in the Mind.

to the condition, character, and capabilities of man is not to be obtained by a reference to only one department of knowledge "—that physiological and moral science must be combined for the purpose; and *secondly*, for the practical purpose of showing to how great an extent we can improve our present faculties.

The form which he adopts is that of the dialogue, the interlocutors being three, Eubulus — the good counsellor—a man of wide culture and still wider sympathies, Ergates, the practitioner and physiologist, who represents Brodie himself, and Crites, a distinguished and enlightened lawyer, whose chief office is to point out objections to or inconsistencies in the opinions of the others.

It seems obvious that the idea and the general plan of these Inquiries are taken from Berkeley's " Alciphron " ; but a comparison between the " Introduction " to each work would show, what a more extended perusal would show more fully, that the imitator is as much inferior in vivacity and dramatic power to his model as Berkeley himself was to the great model of all similar dialogues, Plato. The " Psychological Inquiries " again suffer, in a comparison with " Alciphron," in this respect, that they are vague, and come to no definite conclusion ; while " the Minute Philosopher " is directed to a definite end— the vindication of the reasonableness of Christianity.

The scenery—a country house and park with surrounding hills—is a description of Broome Park—the house where Brodie passed the closing years of his life.

The radical difference between Brodie's psychological **speculations** and the modern school **of** Psychology is that he treats the question of the existence and creative energy **of** God as settled, and teaches that mind and matter are different in their nature, so that mental phenomena cannot be regarded **as** the products of material forces. He holds **that** God has given to man both a mental and a spiritual constitution, with bodily structures which are fitted to serve as organs for the mind, and which are acted on also **by the** impulses, passions, and sufferings of the **soul** ; and further that He has given **to** beasts mental faculties of **the same** kind as **those of** men, however inferior in quality, and has also adapted their bodily organs to the **mental capabilities of** each **animal.** He regards both **the human faculties and the** faculties of animals **as** capable **of improvement by culture** ; the latter, indeed, **only to a limited** extent, while **to the former** he **is so far from putting a limit that he even regards it as** perfectly **possible that** creatures may **be developed out** of men as much superior to the present race as **the** highest of the present race is to the aboriginal savage. He **is** most emphatic **in** asserting that the mental principle in animals is the same as in men—affirming that there is no alternative to this conclusion, unless **we** are to regard the beasts, with Des Cartes, **as automatons,** and sheltering **himself** behind the high authority of Bishop Butler **(p. 367).** **And he** regards **it as** nearly certain that beasts **have a** language, intelligible amongst themselves, and suited for such purposes as are compatible with their limited mental powers.

With respect to **the** evolutionary theory, which **was**

just then beginning to occupy the attention of the
scientific world and to seize hold of the popular imagination, he expresses no decided conviction, except that
whatever view we hold ought to be formed on scientific
grounds only, and that religious considerations do not
in any way apply to the controversy. He earnestly
protests against the importation of religion into
scientific questions, and especially against the idea
that there is anything atheistic in the evolution
theory "first propounded by the elder Darwin, and
afterwards by Lamarck and the author of the 'Vestiges
of Creation'" (p. 361).

And in many respects he is obviously disposed to
accept the principle of evolution, while he acutely
points out many of the difficulties in the teaching of
Charles Darwin, as follows :—He refers, in the person
of Ergates, to the great changes which animals of
various species and some races of men have been
known to undergo—a fact well known to breeders of
dogs, and illustrated by Mr. Darwin's experiments on
pigeons ; but Darwin, he says, has overlooked the
important fact that all these variations have been only
in the external form—"the transformations do not
extend to the internal and more important vital
organs, nor to the muscles, or even the general form
of the skeleton"—and the animals, however much
altered, seem always to have a tendency to return to
their original type. The main argument (to his
mind) for the theory is that all the various forms of
animals seem to have been framed on a common
pattern ; yet there are organs "which seem to have

no prototype, and which suddenly appear in a limited number of animals as if by some special act of the creative powers." He instances the poison fangs and poison glands of snakes, the electric apparatus of the torpedo and other fishes, and the spinning apparatus of spiders. In fine, he says that he can form no opinion of the subject. Eubulus then remarks on the complication of this problem by the superaddition, as we ascend the animal scale, of mental faculties to the merely animal functions, and the further addition in the human race of a sense of moral responsibility. It seems impossible that these should be developed out of a primordial germ, or out of any material elements (pp. 362–365).

Perhaps the most striking feature in Brodie's psychology is the great importance which he attributes to the imagination, and the training of it by education. From the beginning of the book to the end he labours to show that men live in the world of the imagination as much and as truly as they do in the world of sense —that this faculty, by which the mind recalls, arranges, and selects the objects which have been fixed in it by attention, and then reproduces them— perhaps in some work of art, perhaps in a scientific theory, perhaps in some far-reaching plan of action— is equally important to the highest artist or the loftiest statesman, and to the humblest workman or peasant. The possession of this great faculty he regards as distinguishing man from the lower creatures " While other creatures," he says, "seem to be wholly occupied with the objects which are actually before them, or impelled to the pursuit of those more distant by the force of instinct, man is an imaginative animal" (p. 266). He traces, as a psychologist necessarily must, the faculties of the mind from the first glimmerings of instinct up to the highest achievements of reason, and tries to connect these faculties with the bodily organisation; but he differs with many of our modern physiologists and men of science in regarding the nervous system as being only the organ of the mind, however necessary an organ it may be, "*A priori*, we have no more right," he says, "to say that the brain makes the mind than that the mind makes the brain" (p. 365). Yet he admits, as fully as the most "advanced" modern psychologist could require, the intimate dependence of all our mental processes on the condition of the bodily organs, and *vice versâ* the extent to which the latter are probably affected by all the various conditions of the former.[1] Only, in his view, as the brain makes use of the muscles for motion, or of the eye for the transmission of visual perceptions; so does the mind use the brain for collecting the material of thought or transmitting its mandates to the various parts of the body.[2]

This philosophy rests, as all philosophies must rest, on an unproved assumption, for at the root of every system of psychology or any other science, there are, either expressed or implied, certain "axioms," as Euclid called them. Brodie's axiom is

[1] See Appendix O, Physical Changes in Nervous System from Mental Action.

[2] Brodie quotes Newton as saying, "The organs of sense are not for enabling the soul to perceive the species of things in its sensorium, but only for conveying them thither."

that "the existence of one's own mind[1] is the only thing of which one has any positive and actual knowledge" (p. 138). From this assumption he deduces the entire difference in kind of the percipient being from the things which he perceives, or the organs by means of which he perceives them; for Brodie entirely denies that the brain perceives anything. As the eye does not see, but transmits the visual rays to the brain, so he holds that the brain does not see, but transmits the sense-impressions to the mind.

As, however, the organs of the body are the necessary instruments both for perception and action, it is essential that they should be in right order, and hence the extreme importance which is here attributed to bodily health, and everything by which it is promoted and ensured—temperance, pure air, exercise, sanitary precautions, cheerfulness, healthy activity of all sorts. On this subject he speaks with his usual lucidity and absence of pretension. After alluding with some contempt to the treatises on diet published by certain medical authors, he sums up the experience of a long life spent in the most active practice of one branch of medicine in these few very simple rules: "A reasonable indulgence, without the abuse, of the animal instincts; a life spent in a wholesome atmosphere, and as much as possible in the open air, with a

---

[1] He does not of course imply that we know anything beyond the fact that our mind exists. I have no doubt that he would have agreed with H. Spencer that the nature of the mind neither is nor can be known. He would, in fact, have regarded the question as lying beyond the reach of our faculties and the speculation as useless.

due amount of muscular exercise. Really there is little more to say " (p. 319). How refreshingly does this plain summary of a great surgeon's medical experiences contrast with the pseudo-scientific utterances of some medical authors, or the pompous pretensions of so-called " scientists " ! At the same time he inculcates the extreme importance, even in regard to the bodily health, of keeping the mind sound and cultivating cheerfulness, contentment, and those moderate views of life which will obviate disappointment and despair.[1]

The account given of the mental functions is at any rate intelligible. He begins with instinct—this being defined as " a principle by which animals are induced, independently of experience and reasoning, to the performance of certain voluntary acts, which are necessary to their preservation or the continuance of their species " (p. 213). He proves the reality of such instinctive actions, and that they are not (as some authors contend), all really derived from experience, though he admits that some acts, originally instinctive, may pass into habits, which now appear to us the results of experience.[2] "It is in the proportion," he says, " which their instincts and intelligence bear to each other, that the difference between the minds

[1] See Appendix P, What to expect of Life.

[2] I presume that Brodie had not seen the exceedingly ingenious chapter on Instinct in H. Spencer's "Psychology," with its parallel between instinctive and reflex action ; otherwise I think he would have noticed it in this place. The first edition of Spencer's work was published in 1855, several years before Brodie's " Inquiries " were finally given to the world.

of men and animals chiefly consists " (p. 215). The chief physical differences between men and animals are (1) the erect posture of the former, which enables them to make use of the upper extremity for the various uses to which the human hand is suited ; and (2) the possession of articulate speech—for speech of some sort, and some other means of communicating with each other, he does not regard as wanting to many, perhaps any, of the lower animals. To these instinctive faculties are superadded those of the intellect, rising higher and higher as we ascend the scale of creation ; for it is one of the strongest points in Brodie's psychology that the mental faculties of men and animals are similar in kind, however much the human mind excels in degree. But in man there is also superadded to the mental faculties the sense of moral responsibility—the faculties of the soul. It seems to him impossible that these higher faculties should be developed out of a primordial germ, or out of any material elements whatever. In fact, he regards all the faculties of men and animals, equally with all the properties of the inorganic universe, as the direct results of creative energy, working towards a conscious purpose, whether that energy has worked on the plan of separate creation or gradual development.

As this is an important point in the work I will quote his words :—" It is probable that, in some of the very lowest forms of animal life, the functions, such as they are, are performed automatically, and there is no reason to believe that these simple creatures are endowed with anything like sensation and volition, any more than vegetables. But as we ascend in the scale of animal life, we find another principle super-added—a principle which even in worms and insects is the subject of sensation and volition, and which, as we ascend still higher in the scale, we find endowed with the faculties of memory, imagination, and thought, attaining their highest degree of perfection, with the addition of a sense of moral responsibility, in the human race. . . . In some modern works on Physi-ology, I see the mind spoken of as one of the properties (or, as they now call it, forces) inherent in matter, corresponding to gravitation, electricity, magnetism, and so on. . . . But this is a doctrine which I cannot easily accept. I cannot perceive the smallest analogy between the processes of mind, and what are called forces inherent in the molecules of matter. There is so wide a gulf between them that one can in no way be compared with the other. I have no conception of any form of matter which is not essentially and infinitely divisible ; the only thing of which I have any knowledge, which is essentially indivisible, is my own mind. The materials of the body, including those which compose the brain, are in a state of constant change. . . . But amid these changes the mind preserves its identity. The belief in the identity of my own mind is as much inherent in me, and as much a part of my constitution, as my belief in the existence of an external world ; I can in no way emancipate myself from it " (pp. 364, 365).

In all this there is nothing new,[1] nor does Brodie set before himself any such aim as to found a new school, or to give a new explanation of the riddle of the universe. Highly as he thought of the imagination, and eloquent as he is in pointing out its leading place amongst all our faculties, he is careful in these "inquiries" to limit himself strictly to facts. In the physical sciences, he says, even erroneous hypotheses have a substance and reality on which new progress can be based ; but in psychology "we soon arrive where our knowledge ends, while, if we endeavour to overleap this boundary, we pass at once into a region of mists and shadows, where the greatest intellects do but grope their way to no good purpose, striving to know the unknowable, and speculating on subjects beyond their reach" (p. 270) ; and in another passage he dwells on the necessity for "another quality for which he can find no other English name than that of humility, though that does not exactly express the meaning,[2] that quality which leads a man to look into himself, to find out his own deficiencies and endeavour to correct them, to doubt his own observations until they are carefully verified, to doubt also his own con-clusions until he has looked at them on every side, and considered all that has been urged, or that might be

---

[1] "Commonplace, after all," says Mr. John Morley, "is exactly what contains the truths that are indispensable" (Romanes' Lecture on Macchiavelli, p. 21).

[2] It seems to me exactly expressed by the Greek word σωφροσύνη. Brodie's teaching is but the echo of a greater teacher—μὴ ὑπερφρονεῖν παρ' ὃ δεῖ φρονεῖν, ἀλλὰ φρονεῖν εἰς τὸ σωφρονεῖν (Rom. xii. 3).

urged against them. . . . In this sense of the word the greatest men are humble " (p. 295).

It is in this spirit that he " inquires " into the great faculties which have been attributed to the mind, though, as he justly says, " Writers class the mental faculties as if they were absolutely distinct from each other. . . . But in reality those different conditions of the mind, to which we give the name of the mental faculties, are so mixed up together, no one of them can be said ever to exist separately " (p. 311).

I have tried to give, in the above, a short account of the main features of Brodie's system, so far as he can be said to have laid down any system, of psychology ; but it is not set forth in that order, nor indeed set forth at all. The dialogues are mainly discourses upon the various attributes and states of the mind, and the influences which act on them, and, as dialogues are apt to do, they wander about—starting, from some accidental connection, with the consideration of some topic which has no reference to what precedes, and often coming back to one which has been treated of before. Much is said about sleep and dreams—the memory occupies much of the attention of the inquirers ; they speculate whether there is a separate organ in the brain for this faculty, what the uses of memory are, how it should be cultivated, how it serves imagination and supplies it with material, yet how useless the most retentive memory is in itself, unless " founded on the relations which objects and events have to each other, one suggesting another, so that they present themselves, not as insulated facts, but as parts of a whole" (p. 292). Of the high place which is assigned to imagination among the human faculties I have spoken above ; and it is a topic to which the interlocutors lovingly return over and over again, and which is illustrated in some of the best passages in these dialogues. Instinct, again, occupies a great space in the book ; and not only are the bodily instincts treated of, but those of the mind also, as the social and the religious instincts. There are many interesting reflections on the condition of the early races of men, and in a long note (on p. 381) the author dwells on the great importance, at the time, of inventions which are now so familiar that they attract no notice—flint weapons, the domestication of the dog, the use of wheels—but, above all, the use of fire for smelting, cooking, and a thousand other purposes. He conjectures that the knowledge of the use of fire may not have been founded on experience at all ; but on a special instinct implanted in man for that purpose. The higher faculties of the soul also occupy much of the attention of the interlocutors. A scholar of Bishop Butler might indeed have been expected to say more of the conscience considered separately ; but no doubt it is included in what he says about moral responsibility and about free-will. On the latter subject he declines to enter at any length, merely observing that if metaphysical argument seems to be on the side of necessity, irresistible conviction is on the other ; and the practical result of the necessitarian doctrine is really *nil*—no one, when he quits the loftier regions of metaphysics, acts otherwise than as if he believed in free-will.[1]

So careful an observer of life and of all its functions could not but have studied death with equal care and minuteness. It is consoling to find one so familiar with death in all its forms saying (in the character of Ergates, who, it will be remembered, personifies Brodie himself) that he " had never known but two instances in which, in the act of dying, there were manifest indications of the fear of death." As to this, however, I believe that the universal authority of medical men would endorse what Milton says, that the many ways that lead to Death's grim cave, though all dismal, yet are "to sense more terrible at the entrance than within." [2] He also produces instances (especially a very notable one of Dr. Wollaston) to show that it is most probable that even in the stupor of approaching death the soul retains its power, although it has lost the bodily organs of expression ; and he thinks the independence of the immaterial from the material part is equally shown by the phenomena of drowning and other states of semi-consciousness — dreams, nightmare, &c.

As the treatise deals so much with the faculties of both body and mind, it is no wonder that a great part

---

[1] The contrast between the wise common sense of this follower of the *a posteriori* method of arguing from facts, and the dogmatic confidence of the " high priori road," may be appreciated by any one who likes to turn to Herbert Spencer's " Psychology," vol. i. p. 503, ed. 1870, and see the trenchant way in which he decides this secular controversy in favour of the Necessitarians.

[2] " Paradise Lost," xi. 468.

of it is occupied by education, the agent by means of which both classes of faculties are to be improved. Of physical education he says little ; its importance is fully admitted, but he thinks that it can well take care of itself, and needs little in the way of express enactments ; but the education of the mind is a theme which is constantly reappearing in these dialogues from the first to the last. Brodie insists most strongly on the indefinite capacity of the human mind for improvement ; though in an interesting note which closes the work he repudiates the extravagant anticipations of Condorcet as to the perfectibility of the human race and the prospect of attaining terrestrial immortality. Yet he seems himself to think not only that the lowest races may in time rise as high as the highest now are, but that "in the revolution of ages some new variety of man may be produced, as superior to the European of the present day as the European is to the Australian savage." Nor does he shrink from hinting that as we see in the past simpler forms of animals succeeded by higher beings, so in the future, when man's mission on earth has been completed, he too may be replaced by other living beings "far superior to him in all the highest qualities with which he is endowed, and holding a still more exalted place in the system of the universe " (p. 378).

Having such high ideas of human destiny, it is no wonder that he should strive to teach his fellows how to "rise on stepping-stones of their dead selves to higher things." He is no educational fanatic. Some persons

of the highest order of intellect, he believes, have probably benefited by being left in early years without
much schooling, as instanced by Davy, John Hunter,
and Ferguson, the astronomer. "A high education
is a leveller which, while it tends to improve ordinary
minds, and to turn idleness into industry, may, in
some instances, have the effect of preventing the full
expansion of genius" (p. 134); and he allows that
uninstructed people may judge as soundly as the
educated. All depends on the original powers of the
mind. There may be much wisdom with little knowledge, and *vice versâ* (p. 292); but though extraordinary
persons may dispense, to a great extent, with teaching,
there are a large number who can only learn what
they are taught (p. 339). Hence it is of the utmost
importance to specify what are the essential objects of
education and the best way of attaining them. Brodie
is not one of those who confound instruction or
learning with education. The object of education
is, he teaches, to arouse the faculties of the soul, and
direct them to high and worthy subjects. Education
should be directed to discipline a child in attention,
industry, and perseverance; to strengthen the memory,
to improve and purify the imagination, to elevate the
moral sentiments, and to inculcate such elementary
principles of religion as a child can comprehend and
put into practice.

To acquire knowledge is in his judgment an essential
part of education; but it should not be regarded as
the only, or even as the principal, object at first.
"The acquirement of knowledge is the instrument

by means of which the intellectual faculties are to be exercised and developed and brought into harmony with each other." And above and before all else, he says, a child ought to be made to understand the value of truth, of telling it and of seeking it—a habit of mind which must be instilled into him by parental precept and example ; and as this home education depends even more on the mother than the father, he dwells on the importance of a higher education for girls than was then in vogue.

In this training of the faculties he attributes the highest rank to the physical sciences. "No study," he says, "so stimulates the imagination as that of the physical phenomena of the universe, and in this every fresh discovery is but the beginning of a further progress. In these studies every variety of the human intellect may find its suitable employment. The discursive imagination of one, the aptitude for arrangement and classification possessed by another, and the mathematical genius of a third, may alike be turned to good account (pp. 266, 267). But he believes that education is best commenced, in the old traditional way, by the study of languages, as the best means of arousing and strengthening the attention, and that for this purpose the dead are superior to living languages as requiring "more thought, more attention, more exercise of memory" (p. 346). Mathematics he regards as less appropriate for training the mind in youth, and he says, rather whimsically, I think, that mathematicians seem rather more disposed than other persons to credulity, for in mathematics there is no "other side" to attend to, "we arrive at a conclusion about which there is no possibility of doubt, or at none at all " (p. 132).

But through all his discussion of the kinds of study to be pursued runs the main idea that the end of study is not the mere acquiring of the knowledge of facts, but the discipline of the soul and of the mental faculties. Various kinds of study will suit various dispositions; but "the pursuit of any kind of knowledge, whatever its ultimate value may prove to be, will, in a greater or less degree, answer the intended purpose" (p. 343). That purpose, in his view, is to acquire the self-control which distinguishes the civilised man from the savage, and so to fit oneself to resist, as far as may be, the overpowering force of circumstances. For Brodie was, above all things, a practical man, and dealt with men and facts as he found them. Therefore he allows, as fully as any "necessarian," the dominance which must always be exercised over human conduct by circumstances, or "the environment," if we wish to speak in the fashionable dialect ; but he is a believer in free-will, and therefore does not hold that a man's circumstances are a sufficient defence for his actions whatever they may be. His aim is the same as that of the old moralist, "Qui Fortunæ te responsare superbæ Liberum et erectum præsens hortatur et aptat." [1]

Old fashioned as all this may seem to the disciples of Mr. Herbert Spencer, I confess that it seems nearer the truth than the philosophy which, like Dante's Semiramis, "Libito fè lecito in sua legge" ("Has

[1] Hor., Ep. I. i. 68

made a law by which you are allowed to do your pleasure ") ; and for my own part Brodie's psychology appears to me not only more in accordance with the facts of life, but more truly scientific than a system, however logical,[1] in whose dreary pages one might wander for ever without finding out that the human soul, which is the subject of the investigation, has any such faculties as imagination, conscience, or affections.

The general theory of education is applied in more than one of the dialogues to the public education of the mass of the people. And here, also, Brodie's sentiments, though liberal, are strictly restrained by what he thinks practicable. While allowing the importance of all knowledge, and the equal right of all men to any advantage they can obtain, he doubts the practicability of giving any but the most rudimentary education to girls and boys of the labouring class, and is not at all disposed to allow the hours of schooling to interfere with those of recreation—for he regards healthy recreation, and everything which improves the bodily health, as being necessary for the health of the mind and the soul—dependent as that is on the healthy condition of the organs of the body.

Another question closely connected with education is whether it increases the sum of happiness in the world or no. Some hold that the uneducated have as much enjoyment of life as the most intellectual.

[1] Never let us forget that a system is not necessarily true because it is logical. Logic is the art of deducing conclusions from premises. If your premises—the axioms of your system—are false, the more logical the system, the farther will you be from the truth.

Crites, therefore, raises the question whether it is not true that increase of knowledge only means increase of pain ? This view is strongly combated by the other interlocutors, Eubulus and Ergates. They maintain, on the contrary, that intellectual advancement promotes civilisation, prolongs the average period of life, and thus increases the general happiness, that term being defined as "the largest proportion of agreeable and the smallest proportion of painful feelings, either physical or moral" (p. 315). A striking apologue of Lucian is adduced to show that this happiness, dependent though it is on the bodily health and the outward circumstances, consists essentially in the condition of the inward feelings—that a certain amount of healthy labour, whether of body or mind, is a necessary preservative against *ennui*, and that "there is really nothing more necessary to the enjoyment of life than constant occupation of mind" (p. 325); that there can be no happiness without society ; that "those who live much alone not only become stupid, but narrow-minded and selfish" (p. 326); and that many form too high expectations of life, such as necessarily lead to disappointment ; so that many persons after amassing large fortunes "become hypochondriacal, partly perhaps from being deprived of their usual occupation, but in a great degree also because they have learned that the object for the attainment of which they had toiled was worth so much less than they had expected" (p. 328). This, however, applies chiefly to men who have spent their lives in acquiring wealth.

Then they turn to the question of good and evil, some one having recalled the myth which Socrates suggests in the "Phædo" as illustrative of the fact that pleasure and pain always follow closely on each other, and they seem on the point of falling into the endless speculations about the origin of evil, when Crites suggests that these subjects are above our faculties, and they turn to the more practical subject whether good or evil predominates in the world. On this Brodie speaks with no uncertain voice. For himself he says he cannot but believe "that the good greatly predominates over the evil, and that the individual cases in which it is otherwise are but rare exceptions to the general rule" (p. 330). And, he adds, there is much good which we enjoy, but which we take for granted and rarely notice. He allows, of course, that the difference in the answers given to this question by different persons depends mainly on their different circumstances : and Brodie had himself been so prosperous that he would naturally incline to the cheerful view. But we must remember that this passage was written, or at least published, in his last year, when all that prosperity was over and his life was closing in solitude and pain and darkness.

It is, however, taking too narrow a view of the world to think of man only. The earth teems with life, even where man cannot penetrate. Are these creatures happy or no? He believes they are, that their habitual condition is one of present enjoyment, that they have little recollection of what is past and very limited anticipations of the future (p. 331).

Their speculations on the healthy mind naturally lead them to consider the mind diseased. Much of interest will be found in these Dialogues on the states of mind associated with the circulation of impure blood through the brain, as in drunkenness and other intoxication, drowning, and similar states of asphyxia [1] (on which Brodie had worked so much and so well), and various derangements of the general health—some of these producing a transient, others a permanent, change in the functions or the composition of the nervous system. He admits that these facts demonstrate that insanity can be, and is often, produced by a change in the brain, though in these conditions he believes that the mind also acts on the brain. But he teaches that insanity may also depend on mental causes only—the brain having been entirely unaffected till it fell under the dominion of the diseased mind or soul. And this of course introduces the subject of "Moral Insanity," in which there are supposed to be no illusions nor any affection of the intellect, but simply a perversion of the moral sentiments. The idea that there is such a form of insanity, and that it exempts the patient from responsibility and from punishment is decidedly repudiated here ; but the subject is perhaps too technical for discussion in these pages. I would only subjoin as an instance of Brodie's freedom from professional priggishness his conclusion on the whole

---

[1] The close analogy between drowning and intoxication is put strongly by Tennyson in "Despair"—

"Visions of youth—for my brain was drunk with the water, it seems ;
I had passed into perfect quiet at length out of pleasant dreams."

matter. "It is a great mistake to suppose that this is a question which can be determined only by medical practitioners. Any one of plain common sense, and having a fair knowledge of human nature, who will give it due consideration, is competent to form an opinion on it" (p. 172).

Scattered up and down the work are numerous instances of its author's practical wisdom and scientific foresight. Thus, he gives instances (pp. 143, 144) of aphasia, congenital and acquired, to show that there must be an organ of speech somewhere in the brain, the injury or malformation of which produces more or less complete loss of speech, irrespective of any concomitant loss of other functions. Broca's localisation of this organ in 1861 [1] confirmed this forecast of Brodie. And in speaking of congenital deafness he notices that a child under his observation by "a close attention to the motion of the lips (and, as I presume, by observing those smaller movements of the features which are unnoticed by others) was enabled to obtain a competent knowledge not, indeed, of what her mother said, but of what she meant to say" (p. 282), an observation which contains the germ of the subsequent introduction of "lip-reading." [2]

Long before the depletion of the agricultural districts had become a topic for newspaper discussion Brodie had remarked it, and deplores it in more than

[1] "Broca sur le siège de la faculté de langage."

[2] Lip-reading, if I may trust my memory, had gone out of use and notice in England at this period—but it was still employed abroad, especially in Germany. Wallis, the distinguished mathematician, then

one passage of these dialogues. And long before any one had been raised to the peerage on account of eminence in science, he pointed out the danger to the love of science for its own sake which might be involved in a connection between eminence in science and worldly advancement.

And the whole work is impregnated throughout with that love of noble literature, and of all things "lovely and of good report," which is the natural result of good discipline in youth and high aspirations strenuously followed during a long life of honourable exertion.

Professor at Oxford, exhibited to Charles II., in 1662, a deaf and dumb person whom he had taught to speak and write. This person was not congenitally deaf, but had lost his hearing at the age of five. He speaks, however, of a congenital deaf-mute whom he had taught to speak ("Phil. Trans.," 1698. See also Hartmann, "Taubstummheit," &c. Stuttgart, 1880, ch. xiv.).

FINIS.

APPENDICES

APPENDIX A.

Brodie on the Choice of a Profession.

(See page 28.)

"I know that it often happens that a young man is brought up to a particular profession, because it is supposed that he has an especial liking for it, or a 'particular turn that way.' Now I do not say that this goes for nothing, and I have no doubt that one structure of mind may, on the whole, be better adapted for one pursuit and another for another. But I also know that in many instances there is nothing beyond a mere love of novelty; and I have very much more confidence in those who enter a profession after due thought and reflection, with a strong determination that, having done so, they will not fail from want of attention, and that they will create for themselves a feeling of interest in it."

(Vol. i. p. 514, "Intr. Disc.," 1846.)

APPENDICES

APPENDIX B.

I have found, among Sir Benjamin's papers, the MSS. of two essays read at this Academical Society in the year 1802, one "On the Principles of Science," and the other, "An Enquiry into the Justice of the Prejudices commonly entertained against Metaphysical Speculations." He was right in not having them published, for they contain nothing which even at that time was new ; but they are interesting to a biographer, as showing that the strong masculine sense, and the lucidity which characterise all Brodie's writings, were acquired (as such characters must be acquired by all but men of the greatest genius) by profound study of the best authors and ordered meditation on such study. The first deals with the difference between the inductive and deductive methods, and the utility of "working hypotheses," as they are now called, though Brodie does not use the term. The second shows how persistent was his devotion to the metaphysical sciences, and is in itself remarkable for the very elevated idea which the young metaphysician had formed of education—and that at a time when the tendency to confound reading and writing with the education which reading and writing are intended to promote was even stronger than it is at present. When we find the essayist arguing that " the discoveries of Locke are not the less certain because they were followed by the whimsical notions of Kant," we may perhaps wonder whether he had bestowed that care in reading the German which he certainly had given to the study of the English philosopher. The essay seems also defective in that it does not recognise the inferiority of metaphysical to physical theories due to the uncertain nature of the facts on which the former rest.

Another paper, somewhat posterior to these in date ("March or April, 1806") has also been preserved by its author. It is a tract, or a portion of a tract, on some alleged errors in Pliny's "Natural History," and aims at showing that Pliny the Elder was less untrustworthy as a naturalist than he is generally accounted. The paper is no doubt creditable to the taste and reading of a very young medical man ; but it can hardly be intended as the basis of a serious argument. It shows that some of the marvellous things which Pliny relates he does not vouch for, but only puts them on record, and that some of the explanations which he gives of natural phenomena (such as the tides and the rainbow) are not inconsistent with the true theories which science has now established. But the youthful advocate trusts a little too much to the ignorance of his audience when he proceeds to argue that Pliny's statement, "Ex fæminis mutari in mares non est fabulosum," is analogous to Hunter's observation that the females of different animals, as they grow older, lose some of the characteristics of their own sex and acquire those of the male. And he passes over the fact that Pliny professes to have seen an instance of change of sex.

APPENDIX C.

BRODIE ON SURGICAL NOTE-TAKING.

(See page 38.)

"It is not by going through the form of walking round the wards daily with the physician and surgeon, that you will be enabled to avail yourselves of the opportunities of obtaining knowledge, which the hospital affords. You should investigate cases for yourselves ; you should converse on them with each other ; you should take written notes of them in the morning, which you may transcribe in the evening ; and in doing so you should make even what are regarded as the more trifling cases the subject or reflection. Some individuals are more, others less, endowed by nature with the power of reflection ; but there are none in whom the faculty may not be improved by exercise, and whoever neglects it is unfitted for the medical profession. You will be at once sensible of the great advantage arising from your written notes of cases. But that advantage is not limited to the period of your education. Hereafter, when these faithful records of your experience have accumulated, you will find them to be an important help in your practice."

(Vol i. p. 471, "Introductory Discourse at St. George's," October 1, 1838. See also vol. i. p. 535, Address on delivering Prizes in 1850.)

APPENDIX D.

Brodie on the Prize System.

(See page 39.)

In the evidence given by Sir Benjamin Brodie before a public commission, he says : "I have much doubt myself about giving competitive prizes in examinations. It may work well in schools and colleges ; but when you come to professional examinations, I do not think that competitive prizes will answer ; for after all they will be obtained chiefly by those who are crammed, by the men of good memories, and not by those who work. It seems to me that the man who thinks will not have the advantage that he ought to have. I would limit the prizes to one class, founded on cases. I believe the ordinary prizes do very little good. . . . These prizes operate in this manner. A man wants a prize. He gets books, reads up the subject ; and this kind of work keeps him out of the dissecting room and the wards of the hospital. Yet these are the only places where he can get any knowledge that he can apply to practice, and learn to observe and think."

(Vol. i. p. 538, *note*.)

APPENDIX E.

Brodie as a Medical Reviewer.

(See page 57.)

I have taken the trouble of looking up these reviews, and find that they justify the opinion expressed in the text. Brodie's style of reviewing is trenchant and severe. This was a general characteristic of reviewing in the days of Jeffrey, Gifford, and Lockhart ; but he speaks as one having both knowledge and authority. In reviewing the "Anatomist's Vade Mecum," he expresses the contempt which he felt for dissecting-books, in comparison with actual work by the hands of the student himself. And in his review of Cooper's Dictionary he speaks hardly less contemptuously of "Systems" of Surgery, saying also (and I think with truth) that the alphabetical arrangement of such works, followed in that Dictionary, is the worst possible. The main contention of the article on Allan's work on Lithotomy is that though a competent operator can perform lithotomy quite safely with a common knife, yet the "cutting gorget" of Sir Cæsar Hawkins (which is a special form of knife with a beak) is a preferable instrument on the whole. This was not the conclusion to which their subsequent experience led Sir Cæsar's successors at St. George's, where the cutting gorget had become antiquated before my time.

On the whole, the articles do no discredit even to a man of Brodie's high standing, considered as juvenile performances.

APPENDIX F.

ROUX'S " RELATION D'UN VOYAGE FAIT À LONDRES EN 1814."

(See page 74.)

Those who care to turn back to a book dating from

the year of Waterloo will be well repaid by a glance at this work of Roux. Brodie is frequently and honourably mentioned in it. Roux relates how he demonstrated to Brodie Desault's method of applying a ligature to the neck of a nasopharyngeal polypus, and how skilfully Brodie carried out the operation. He gives a long account of the cases in which Brodie used the seton in the treatment of ununited fracture ; and he speaks in terms of praise of his then published works on the Diseases of Joints—though his praise is faint, and he finally damns the work by describing it as consisting of "observations desquelles il a tiré des conséquences plus ingénieuses qu'utiles." But Brodie's work had not then progressed far enough to vindicate its far reaching influence on surgery. The book is a charming one, and most interesting to surgeons as showing how far even at that time English was ahead of foreign surgery. M. Roux mentions, but hardly dares, he says, to mention, that the English had even conceived the idea that the innominate artery might possibly be tied with success—an imagination which, after many failures, has at last been converted into a reality.

APPENDIX G.

CORRESPONDENCE ABOUT LIEBIG'S CANDIDATURE AT KING'S COLLEGE, LONDON.

(See p. 79.)

"I am glad that you have enjoyed your time (at Prague) and found it a relief from the dulness of

Giessen. However, a dull place is just the place for study, and if Liebig enters the busy theatre of London he must make up his mind to meeting with great impediments to his philosophical pursuits. Engagements of societies, committees, and other people's business of all kinds and sorts—these things interfere vastly with the calm pursuits of science in this great metropolis. Faraday avoids the first of these by never going out anywhere. Herschel has gone away from the whole, and pursues his favourite studies and attends to the education of his children in rural retirement. These things have come into my mind because there is a negotiation going on with Liebig to come to King's College in the place of Daniel, and by the desire of the Professors I have just written to the Bishop of London to know whether a Lutheran Professor will not be as good as one of our own Church Establishment. The rule of the College is that all Professors, except those of modern languages, should belong to the English Church. On the whole it seems to me very doubtful whether the ecclesiastical members of the Council will agree to admit any one who will not subscribe to the Thirty-nine Articles."

Sir Benjamin wrote accordingly, and the Bishop (Dr. Blomfield) replied as follows :—

"LONDON HOUSE,
"*May* 6, 1845.
"MY DEAR SIR BENJAMIN,—I am quite aware

233

of the advantages which King's College would derive from the appointment of such a man as Professor Liebig to the Chair of Chemistry, but the express words of the Charter appear to me to present an insuperable bar to such appointment. Whether right or wrong, there they stand in the Charter; and if any appeal were made to the visitor against the appointment of any Professor not being a member of the Church of England, it would be his duty to declare the election null and void. The instance of Professor Ferguson has been quoted, but there is obviously a material distinction between the two; and if there were not, I should say that if we have clearly disregarded the express terms of the Charter in one instance we should be all the more careful not to do so a second time. The well-being of our College depends most materially on a strict adherence to the principles upon which it was founded, and of a departure from which every subscriber to the College would have a right to complain. I have consulted the Archbishop on the subject, who takes the same view of it as myself.

"Believe me,
"My dear Sir Benjamin,
"Yours very truly,
"C. J. LONDON."

APPENDICES

APPENDIX H.

(On page 110.)

LETTERS TO BRODIE ON HIS APPOINTMENT AS
SERJEANT-SURGEON.

Windsor Castle,
September 2, 1832.

SIR,—I have been honoured with the King's com-
mands to acquaint you that his Majesty, having been
made aware of the intention expressed often by his
late brother, King George the IVth, to confer upon
you the situation of Serjeant-Surgeon, if it should
become vacant, in consideration of your attendance
upon his Majesty during his illness—has considered
it due to the memory of his late Majesty as well as
to the meritorious services which it had been his
wish so to reward, to carry his intentions into effect.

His Majesty has, therefore, ordered me to communicate to you his pleasure that you should succeed
to the situation of Serjeant-Surgeon to his Majesty,
which has become vacant by the death of Sir Everard
Home.

I have the honour to be, sir,
Your most obedient humble servant,
H. TAYLOR.

September 5, 1832.

DEAR MR. BRODIE,—I thank you for the favour
of your friendly letter. The announcement of your
appointment as Serjeant-Surgeon I may reckon
among the very few things that have given me

pleasure since the death of his late Majesty. I am glad of this appointment, not only as regards your own merits but on many other accounts which I will not enumerate. As I am now secluded from the world it is not likely that the opportunity of our seeing each other will often occur; but I have a kindred feeling with yourself, in looking back to those days that are passed away, when our mutual confidence made us feel the value of that intercourse which I shall always remember with pleasure and satisfaction.—Always yours most sincere and faithful friend,

W. Knighton.

APPENDIX I.

Brodie on Making Money.

(On page 127.)

"To obtain such a competency as will place your-selves and your families above the reach of want, and enable you to enjoy such of the comforts and advan-tages of life as usually fall to the lot of persons in the same station as yourselves is undoubtedly one of your first duties, and one of the principal objects to which your attention should be directed ; but nevertheless let it never be forgotten that it forms but a part, and a small part, of professional success.

(Vol. i., p. 503, " Intro. Disc.", 1843).

APPENDICES

APPENDIX K.

BRODIE ON THE VIS MEDICATRIX NATURÆ

(See page 164.)

" There are too many cases in which the patient's
condition is so manifestly hopeless that it is impossible
for you to overlook it. Let me, however, caution you
that you do not, in any instance, arrive too hastily at
this conclusion. Our knowledge is not so absolute
and certain as to prevent even well-informed persons
being occasionally mistaken on this point. . . . A
sanguine mind, tempered by a good judgment, is the
best for a medical practitioner. [This seems a reminiscence of Sir Everard Home, see p. 103.] Those
who from physical causes or habit are of a desponding
character, will sometimes abandon a patient to a speedy
death whom another would have preserved altogether,
or for a considerable time."

" There is another inquiry which should always be
made before you determine on the adoption of a particular method of treatment. What will happen, in
this case, if no remedies whatever be employed ? . . .
The animal system is not like a clock or a steam-
engine, which being broken you must send to the
clockmaker or engineer to mend it ; and which cannot
be repaired otherwise. The living machine, unlike
the works of human invention, has the power of
repairing itself ; it contains within itself its own engi-

neer, who for the most part requires no more than some very slight assistance at our hands. . . .

" When I tell you that we are to trust to nature, I do not mean to say that we are to confide in her implicitly, but that our rule should be not to disturb her operations without an adequate reason for so doing. When we know not what to do, it is better that we should do nothing."

("Introductory Discourse," 1838, vol. i. p. 474–78.)

APPENDIX L.

BRODIE ON SELF-RESPECT.

(See page 173.)

" Integrity and generosity of character ; the disposition to sympathise with others ; the power of commanding your own temper, of resisting your selfish instincts ; and that self-respect, so important in every profession, but especially so in our own profession, which would prevent you from doing in secret what you would not do before all the world ; these things are rarely acquired, except by those who have been careful to scrutinise and regulate their own conduct in the very outset of their career."

(" Introductory Discourse," 1843, vol. i. p. 487.)

BRODIE ON SELF-HELP.

" Those who are well-disposed to you cannot help you unless you first help yourselves. But let me not be mistaken. It is well to be conscious that you are to rely on yourselves alone ; and that even if you were base enough to cringe and stoop for the purpose of obtaining the favour of others, you could derive no permanent advantage from it. This is the independence which I mean, and not that proud and misanthropical independence which rejects the feeling of all obligations to others. Whoever gives you his good opinion, whatever his station in life may be, is in some measure to be considered as conferring an obligation on you, and deserves to be regarded by you with kindness in return. Mankind are bound to each other by mutually receiving and conferring benefits. . . . As others will lean upon you, you must be content to lean upon them."

("Introductory Discourse," 1843, vol. i. p. 501.)

APPENDIX M.

BRODIE'S ACCOUNT OF SIR R. PEEL'S CASE.

(See page 175.)

[What follows is copied from Sir Benjamin Brodie's papers, and is in his words.]

"The account given by M. Guizot of the effects of the injury which occasioned Sir Robert Peel's death is very inaccurate. The following is a copy of the statement sent to Sir Robert Peel's executors, and which it is, I believe, their intention to publish at some future period.

"'On Saturday, the 29th of June, 1850, as Sir Robert

Peel was riding up Constitution Hill in the Green Park, he was thrown from his horse; the fall was evidently accidental in consequence of the horse having either swerved on one side or stumbled. It has been suggested that he was seized with some kind of fit, but at no period of his life had he ever been subject to attacks of that character and there is not the least reason to suspect that he had been thus affected on this occasion. He was taken up in a state of extreme suffering and faintness ; Sir James Clark, who was near the spot at the time, had him placed in a carriage and conveyed to his residence in Whitehall Gardens.

"When surgical assistance was obtained he was found to be still in a state of collapse and faintness ; at the same time expressing most intense pain which was so much aggravated by every attempt to examine the nature of the injury as to render the examination very difficult. It was, however, plain that the principal mischief was in the neighbourhood of the left shoulder there being a comminuted fracture of the clavicle with a perceptible enlargement of the parts below that bone and under the pectoral muscle which could be attributed to nothing but an extensive effusion of blood in this situation. No other injury during life could be distinctly ascertained ; but a severe pain felt in the back part of the chest made it not improbable that there was a fracture of the ribs in addition to that of the clavicle.

"Some bandages were applied round the chest, fixing the arm to the side with a view to support and prevent the movement of the injured parts. These, however, instead of giving relief aggravated the patient's suffering; and he became so disturbed and restless in consequence that, after some time, it was necessary to remove them and trust altogether to keeping the parts quiet by placing him in the recumbent position with the arms supported by a pillow. The state of faintness and collapse which immediately followed the accident continued, so that any attempt to give relief by the abstraction of blood was out of the question.

"Indeed, there seemed to be some danger of the action of the heart failing altogether, so that it was necessary in the first intance to have recourse only to those remedies which might help to maintain the circulation and diminish suffering.

"On the following day there was no material improvement. The enlargement below the clavicle had increased, forming a swelling which could barely be covered with the hand. After some time it was observed that the swelling not only pulsated synchronously with the action of the heart, but (when examined carefully by the eye) that there was another movement perceptible in it, which seemed to correspond to the contractions of the auricle of the heart, resembling what may be seen in the veins of the neck in some very thin persons. From these circumstances there was sufficient reason to believe that there was a communication between the extravasated blood which caused the swelling and some large vein, and that the hæmorrhage itself was the consequence of the subclavian vein having been lacerated by the splinters of the fractured bone, the pulsation being caused by the contiguity of the heart on one side and of the subclavian and axillary artery on the other. From the size of the swelling it was plain that the effusion of blood was very extensive, and sufficient to explain the faintness and collapse which immediately followed the accident and from which there was never anything more than a partial recovery afterwards. The extent of this effusion also explained (by the pressure which it made on the large nerves in the arm-pit) the exceeding pain which existed in the immediate neighbourhood of the injury as well as two other symptoms which were observed afterwards, namely, a sense of numbness and a partially paralytic state of the muscles of the hand and forearm.

"The state of prostration was such that at no period was it possible to venture on any considerable abstraction of blood. On one occasion, when there was some improvement in the state of the circulation fifteen leeches were applied in the neighbourhood of the shoulder, but even the moderate loss of blood which these occasioned was followed by such a degree of exhaustion as made it necessary to administer wine and other stimulants.

"On the 1st of July, in addition to the other symptoms, there was a violent and frequent cough, and the pulse, which on the previous day had been only eighty, rose to ninety, and then to a hundred in a minute. With a view to arrest inflammation, and as the only means of doing so, an active mercurial treatment was begun and persevered in as long as there seemed to be any probability of its being useful.

"In the early part of Tuesday, the 2nd of July (the third day from that of the accident), there was some apparent improvement, but it was only for a short time, and on the evening of that day Sir Robert Peel gradually sunk and died at eleven o'clock.

"It was ascertained after death that there had been a fracture of one or more ribs underneath the left scapula. By desire of the family no examination of the body was made after death. Although Sir Robert Peel had generally enjoyed good health, he had been of a gouty habit. It is also worthy of notice that previously to the accident he had been in a state which rendered him peculiarly sensitive as to bodily pain ; and this may in part explain the greatness of his sufferings on this last occasion. A few weeks before the accident occurred he received a blow on the hand, which had been suddenly pressed against the bars of an enclosure while patting a goat in the Zoological Gardens, and even this small injury occasioned an attack of faintness which lasted a considerable time."

[MEM.—I do not find that this statement was ever published *in extenso*, but its substance must have been communicated to the *Lancet*, for many of its most essential particulars are reproduced in Sir Benjamin's own words in an article in that paper of July 6, 1850.]

APPENDICES

APPENDIX N.

BRODIE ON A SELF-REGULATING PRINCIPLE IN THE MIND.

(See page 202.)

" The first effect usually produced on the mind of a medical student is that of being bewildered by the number and variety of subjects to which his attention is directed. . . . But have patience for a while ; keep your attention fixed on the matters which are brought before you . . . and in the course of a short time there will be an end of the confusion. . . . As you acquire a more extensive knowledge of individual facts, it must necessarily happen that the relations which they bear to each other will become more distinctly developed. This, however, does not seem to be the whole explanation. I cannot well understand what I have observed to happen in myself without supposing that there is in the human mind a principle of order which operates without the mind itself being at the time conscious of it. You have been occupied with a particular investigation ; you have accumulated a large store of facts, but that is all. After an interval of time, and without any further labour, or any addition to your stock of knowledge, you find all the facts you have learned in their proper places, although you are not sensible of having made any effort for the purpose."

(Vol. i. p. 491. "Intr. Disc.," 1843.)

This is practically repeated in " Psychological Inquiries," part i., dialogue i. (vol. i. p. 128).

APPENDICES

APPENDIX O.

BRODIE ON THE PHYSICAL CHANGES IN THE NERVOUS SYSTEM PRODUCED BY MENTAL ACTION.

(See page 207.)

"The changes which the nervous system undergoes from its constant action are looked at under four heads :—

" 1. The immediate action, or the transmission of impressions, which is probably analogous to electricity or magnetism.

" 2. There must be constant molecular changes of disintegration and renewal—so that though the mind preserves its identity, the brain is quite different at different ages.

" 3. Chemical changes must accompany this constant deposition of new substance out of the blood, and reabsorption into it ; and as the brain and the nervous tissues contain more phosphorus than other parts of the body, so the phosphatic diathesis is associated with causes which exhaust the nervous system.

" 4. There must be some more permanent changes in the brain, produced by memory and the association of ideas—but of the nature of these changes we have no notion, and if we had it would not advance our knowledge. We should be just as far from identifying physical and mental phenomena as we are at present. The link between them would still be wanting, and it would be as idle to speculate on the nature of the relation between mind and matter, as on

the proximate cause of gravitation, or of magnetic
attraction and repulsion " (pp. 198–201).

APPENDIX P.

BRODIE'S ESTIMATE OF WHAT TO EXPECT OF LIFE.

(See page 209.)

In his " Introductory Discourse," 1843, he speaks
thus on this subject :—

" Do not begin life with expecting too much of it.
No one can avoid his share of its anxieties and difficulties. You will see persons who seem to enjoy
such advantages of birth and fortune that they can
have no difficulties to contend with ; and some one of
you may be tempted to exclaim, ' How much is their
lot to be preferred to mine ! ' A moderate experience
of the world will teach you not to be deceived by
these false appearances. They have not your difficulties, but they have their own ; and those in whose
path no real difficulties are placed will make difficulties
for themselves. . . . There is no greater happiness in
life than that of surmounting difficulties ; and nothing
will conduce more than this to improve your intellectual faculties, or to make you satisfied with the
situation which you have attained in life, whatever
it may be " (vol. i. p. 496).

INDEX

247

INDEX

Brodie, Sir B. (*continued*)—
Serjeant-Surgeon, 109,
235 ; lectures on surgery
at Windmill Street, 110 ;
at St. George's Hospital,
112 ; quarrel with Dr.
Wilson, Mr. Lane, &c.,
112 ; made a baronet,
124 ; examiner at College
of Surgeons, 128 ; pro-
cures the reform of the
College of Surgeons, 133 ;
Hunterian oration, 134,
137 ; travels abroad, 138 ;
his knowledge of foreign
languages, 138 ; resigns
at St. George's, 139 ;
delivers clinical lectures
after his resignation, 141 ;
his expressions of attachment to St. George's, 142 ;
his life in the country,
144 ; lives at Hampstead
in the summer, 145 ; buys
land in Suffolk, 145 ;
purchase of Broome Park,
Betchworth, 145 ; cul-
mination of his career,
150 ; personal appearance,
150 ; estimate of his published works, 151 ; as a
practitioner, 153, 155,
156 ; a reader of " Pick-
wick," 154 ; presents from

Brodie, Sir B. (*continued*)—
various persons, 154 ; his
medical correspondence,
157 ; his " Psychological
Inquiries," 159 ; becomes
President of the Medical
and Chirurgical Society,
160 ; on " Quacks and
Quackery," 161 ; on
homœopathy, 162 ; on
Vis Medicatrix Naturæ,
164, 237 ; on Mr. Bru-
nel's case, 167 ; action
in the Chambers-Seymour
scandal, 169 ; President
of the Western Medical
and Surgical Society, 171 ;
attends Sir R. Peel after
his fatal accident, 174 ;
presides over Ethnological
Society, 175 ; his evidence
at Palmer's trial, 177 ;
acts as adviser to the
Home Secretary after
Smethurst's trial, 181 ;
presides over section of
Social Science Associa-
tion, 183 ; President of
General Medical Coun-
cil, 185, and of Royal
Society, 187 ; rumours
of a peerage, 187 ; his
addresses at the Royal
Society, 191 ; failing

INDEX

Council, General Medical, 42, 184

Crichton, Sir A., 39

Crites, interlocutor in "Psychological Inquiries," 203

Croft, Sir Richard, 27, 84

Croonian Lecture, 60

Cutler, Mr., 71, 113, 116, 117, 126, 199

D

Darwin, 205

Davy, Sir H., 46, 47, 61

Death, On, 215

Denman, Lord, 26, 144, 149, 154

Denman, Mrs., 20

Derby, Lord, 188

Des Cartes, 204

Dickinson, Dr. Howship, 96, 113, 168, 170

Dilutions, Homœopathic, 163

Doses, Homœopathic, 163

Drowning, Brodie on, 87

Drury, Mr., of Harrow, 77

Dundas, Sir David, 128

E

Education, Brodie on, 68, 216, 220

Education, Medical, Brodie on, 186

Educational statistics at College of Surgeons, 129

Elections, Hospital, 120; committees for, 122

Ennui, 221

Ergates, interlocutor in "Psychological Inquiries," 203

Ethnological Society, 175

Eubulus, interlocutor in "Psychological Inquiries," 203

Evolution, 205

Ewbank, Mr., 91, 101

Examinations, Medical, 46, 129, 130, 131, 132

Examiners at College of Surgeons, 128, 130

F

Fellowship of College of Surgeons, 129, 130, 133, 136

Female education, Brodie on, 68

Foreign travel, 138

Fowke, Mr. J., 157

Free-will, 214

G

George IV., 90, 106; death of, 107

Good or evil, Predominance of, 222

INDEX

INDEX

R

INDEX

INDEX

255

INDEX

BOOKS FOR RECREATION AND STUDY

PUBLISHED BY
T. FISHER UNWIN,
11, PATERNOSTER
BUILDINGS, LON-
DON, E.C. . . . .

SIX-SHILLING NOVELS

In uniform green cloth, large crown 8vo., gilt tops, **6s.**

Effie Hetherington. By ROBERT BUCHANAN. Second Edition.

An Outcast of the Islands. By JOSEPH CONRAD. Second Edition.

Almayer's Folly. By JOSEPH CONRAD. Second Edition.

The Ebbing of the Tide. By LOUIS BECKE. Second Edition.

A First Fleet Family. By LOUIS BECKE and WALTER JEFFERY.

Paddy's Woman, and Other Stories. By HUMPHREY JAMES.

Clara Hopgood. By MARK RUTHERFORD. Second Edition.

The Tales of John Oliver Hobbes. Portrait of the Author. **Second** Edition.

The Stickit Minister. By S. R. CROCKETT. Eleventh Edition.

The Lilac Sunbonnet. By S. R. CROCKETT. Sixth Edition.

The Raiders. By S. R. CROCKETT. Eighth Edition.

The Grey Man. By S. R. CROCKETT.

In a Man's Mind. By J. R. WATSON.

A Daughter of the Fen. By J. T. BEALBY. Second Edition.

The Herb-Moon. By JOHN OLIVER HOBBES. Third Edition.

Nancy Noon. By BENJAMIN SWIFT. Second Edition. With New Preface.

Mr. Magnus. By F. REGINALD STATHAM. Second Edition.

Trooper Peter Halket of Mashonaland. By OLIVE SCHREINER. Frontispiece.

Pacific Tales. By LOUIS BECKE. With Frontispiece Portrait of the Author. Second Edition.

Mrs. Keith's Crime. By Mrs. W. K. CLIFFORD. Sixth Edition. With Portrait of Mrs. Keith by the Hon. JOHN COLLIER, and a New Preface by the Author.

Hugh Wynne. By Dr. S. WEIR MITCHELL. With Frontispiece Illustration.

The Tormentor. By BENJAMIN SWIFT, Author of "Nancy Noon."

Prisoners of Conscience. By AMELIA E. BARR, Author of "Jan Vedder's Wife." With 12 Illustrations.

The Gods, some Mortals and Lord Wickenham. New Edition. By JOHN OLIVER HOBBES.

The Outlaws of the Marches. By Lord ERNEST HAMILTON. Fully illustrated.

The School for Saints: Part of the History of the Right Honourable Robert Orange, M.P. By JOHN OLIVER HOBBES, Author of "Sinner's Comedy,". "Some Emotions and a Moral," "The Herb Moon," &c.

The People of Clopton. By GEORGE BARTRAM.

T. FISHER UNWIN, Publisher,

WORKS BY JOSEPH CONRAD

I.

AN OUTCAST OF THE ISLANDS

Crown 8vo., cloth, **6s.**

"Subject to the qualifications thus disposed of (*vide* first part of notice), 'An Outcast of the Islands' is perhaps the finest piece of fiction that has been published this year, as 'Almayer's Folly' was one of the finest that was published in 1895 . . . Surely this is real romance—the romance that is real. Space forbids anything but the merest recapitulation of the other living realities of Mr. Conrad's invention—of Lingard, of the inimitable Almayer, the one-eyed Babalatchi, the Naturalist, of the pious Abdulla—all novel, all authentic. Enough has been written to show Mr. Conrad's quality. He imagines his scenes and their sequence like a master; he knows his individualities and their hearts; he has a new and wonderful field in this East Indian Novel of his. . . . Greatness is deliberately written; the present writer has read and re-read his two books, and after putting this review aside for some days to consider the discretion of it, the word still stands."—*Saturday Review*

II.

ALMAYER'S FOLLY

Second Edition. Crown 8vo., cloth, **6s.**

"This startling, unique, splendid book."

Mr. T. P. O'CONNOR, M.P.

"This is a decidely powerful story of an uncommon type, and breaks fresh ground in fiction. . . . All the leading characters in the book—Almayer, his wife, his daughter, and Dain, the daughter's native lover—are well drawn, and the parting between father and daughter has a pathetic naturalness about it, unspoiled by straining after effect. There are, too, some admirably graphic passages in the book. The approach of a monsoon is most effectively described. . . . The name of Mr. Joseph Conrad is new to us, but it appears to us as if he might become the Kipling of the Malay Archipelago."—*Spectator.*

11, Paternoster Buildings, London, E.C.   *c*

T. FISHER UNWIN, Publisher,

THE TALES OF JOHN OLIVER HOBBES

With a Frontispiece Portrait of the Author

Second Edition. Crown 8vo., cloth, **6s.**

" The cleverness of them all is extraordinary."—*Guardian.*

" The volume proves how little and how great a thing it is to write a 'Pseudonym.' Four whole 'Pseudonyms' . . . are easily contained within its not extravagant limits, and these four little books have given John Oliver Hobbes a recognized position as a master of epigram and narrative comedy."—*St. James's Gazette.*

" As her star has been sudden in its rise so may it stay long with us ! Some day she may give us something better than these tingling, pulsing, mocking, epigrammatic morsels."—*Times.*

" There are several literary ladies, of recent origin, who have tried to come up to the society ideal ; but John Oliver Hobbes is by far the best writer of them all, by far the most capable artist in fiction. . . . She is clever enough for anything."—*Saturday Review.*

THE HERB MOON

BY

JOHN OLIVER HOBBES

Third Edition, Crown 8vo., cloth, **6s.**

" The jaded reader who needs sauce for his literary appetite cannot do better than buy 'The Herb Moon.'"—*Literary World.*

" A book to hail with more than common pleasure. The epigrammatic quality, the power of rapid analysis and brilliant presentation are there, and added to these a less definable quality, only to be described as charm. . . . 'The Herb Moon' is as clever as most of its predecessors, and far less artificial."—*Athenæum.*

11, Paternoster Buildings, London, E.C.

SOME 3/6 NOVELS

Uniform Edition of MARK RUTHERFORD'S works. Edited by REUBEN SHAPCOTT. Crown 8vo., cloth.

The Autobiography of Mark Rutherford. Fifth Edition.

Mark Rutherford's Deliverance. New Edition.

Miriam's Schooling, and other Papers. By MARK RUTHERFORD. With Frontispiece by WALTER CRANE. Second Edition.

The Revolution in Tanner's Lane.

Catharine Furze: A Novel. By MARK RUTHERFORD. Fourth Edition.

Clara Hopgood. By MARK RUTHERFORD.

"These writings are certainly not to be lightly dismissed, bearing as they do the impress of a mind which, although limited in range and sympathies, is decidedly original."—*Times.*

The Statement of Stella Maberly. By F. ANSTEY, Author of "Vice Versâ." Crown 8vo, cloth.

"It is certainly a strange and striking story."—*Athenæum.*

Ginette's Happiness. Being a translation by RALPH DERECHEF of "Le Bonheur de Ginette." Crown 8vo., cloth.

"Pretty and gracefully told."—*Pall Mall Gazette.*

Silent Gods and Sun-Steeped Lands. By R. W. FRAZER. Second Edition. With 4 full-page Illustrations by A. D. McCORMICK and a Photogravure Frontispiece. Small crown 8vo., cloth.

"Mr. Frazer writes powerfully and well, and seems to have an intimate acquaintance with the sun-steeped land, and the strange beings who people it."—*Glasgow Herald.*

Paul Heinsius. By CORA LYSTER. Crown 8vo., cloth.

"This is an extremely clever and altogether admirable, but not altogether unkindly, anatomisation of Teutonic character."—*Daily Chronicle.*

My Bagdad. By ELLIOTT DICKSON. Illustrated. 8vo., cloth.

"Related with a refreshing simplicity that is certain to approve itself to readers."—*Bookseller.*

Silk of the Kine. By L. McMANUS (C. MacGuire), Author of "Amabel: A Military Romance." Crown 8vo., cloth.

"We have read 'The Silk of the Kine,' from the first page to the last, without missing a single word, and we sighed regretfully when Mr. McManus brought the adventures of Margery MacGuire and Piers Ottley to a close."—*Literary World.*

A Pot of Honey. By SUSAN CHRISTIAN. Crown 8vo., cloth.

"The book is the outcome of a clever mind."—*Athenæum.*

Liza of Lambeth. By W. SOMERSET MAUGHAM. Crown 8vo., cloth.

"An interesting story of life and character in the Surrey-side slums, presented with a great deal of sympathetic humour."—*Daily Chronicle.*

The Twilight Reef, and other Stories. By HERBERT C. McILWAINE. Crown 8vo., cloth.

THE HALF-CROWN SERIES

✦ ✦ ✦

Each Demy 12mo., cloth.

1. **A Gender in Satan.** By RITA.

2. **The Making of Mary.** By JEAN M. MCILWRAITH.

3. **Diana's Hunting.** By ROBERT BUCHANAN.

4. **Sir Quixote of the Moors.** By JOHN BUCHAN.

5. **Dreams.** By OLIVE SCHREINER.

6. **The Honour of the Flag.** By CLARK RUSSELL.

7. **Le Selve.** By OUIDA. 2nd Edition.

8. **An Altruist.** By OUIDA. 2nd Edition.

THE CAMEO SERIES

✦ ✦ ✦

Demy 12mo., half-bound, paper boards, price **3s. 6d.**
Vols. 14-17, **3s. 6d.** *net.*

Also, an Edition de Luxe, limited to 30 *copies, printed on Japan paper. Prices on application.*

1. **The Lady from the Sea.** By HENRIK IBSEN. Translated by ELEANOR MARX AVELING. Second Edition. Portrait.

4. **Iphigenia in Delphi,** with some Translations from the Greek. By RICHARD GARNETT, LL.D. Frontispiece.

5. **Mireio :** A Provençal Poem. By FREDERIC MISTRAL. Translated by H. W. PRESTON. Frontispiece by JOSEPH PENNELL.

6. **Lyrics.** Selected from the Works of A. MARY F. ROBINSON (Mme. JAMES DARMESTETER). Frontispiece.

7. **A Minor Poet.** By AMY LEVY. With Portrait. Second Edition.

8. **Concerning Cats :** A Book of Verses by many Authors. Edited by GRAHAM R. THOMPSON. Illustrated.

9. **A Chaplet from the Greek Anthology.** By RICHARD GARNETT, LL.D.

11. **The Love Songs of Robert Burns.** Selected and Edited, with Introduction, by Sir GEORGE DOUGLAS, Bart. With Front. Portrait.

12. **Love Songs of Ireland.** Collected and Edited by KATHERINE TYNAN.

13. **Retrospect,** and other Poems. By A. MARY F. ROBINSON (Mme. DARMESTETER), Author of "An Italian Garden," &c.

14. **Brand :** A Dramatic Poem. By HENRIK IBSEN. Translated by F. EDMUND GARRETT.

15. **The Son of Don Juan.** By Don JOSÉ ECHEGARAY. Translated into English, with biographical introduction, by JAMES GRAHAM. With Etched Portrait of the Author by Don B. MAURA.

16. **Mariana.** By Don JOSÉ ECHEGARAY. Translated into English by JAMES GRAHAM. With a Photogravure of a recent Portrait of the Author.

17. **Flamma Vestalis,** and other Poems. By EUGENE MASON. Frontispiece after Sir EDWARD BURNE-JONES.

THE MERMAID SERIES

The Best Plays of the Old Dramatists.
Literal Reproductions of the Old Text.

Post 8vo., each Volume containing about 500 pages, and an etched Frontispiece, cloth, **3s. 6d.** *each.*

1. **The Best Plays of Christopher Marlowe.** Edited by HAVELOCK ELLIS, and containing a General Introduction to the Series by JOHN ADDINGTON SYMONDS.

2. **The Best Plays of Thomas Otway.** Introduction by the Hon. RODEN NOEL.

3. **The Best Plays of John Ford.—** Edited by HAVELOCK ELLIS.

4 and 5. **The Best Plays of Thomas Massinger.** Essay and Notes by ARTHUR SYMONS.

6. **The Best Plays of Thomas Heywood.** Edited by A. W. VERITY, Introduction by J. A. SYMONDS.

7. **The Complete Plays of William Wycherley.** Edited by W. C. WARD.

8. **Nero,** and other Plays. Edited by H. P. HORNE, ARTHUR SYMONS, A. W. VERITY, and H. ELLIS.

9 and 10. **The Best Plays of Beaumont and Fletcher.** Introduction by J. ST. LOE STRACHEY.

11. **The Complete Plays of William Congreve.** Edited by ALEX. C. EWALD.

12. **The Best Plays of Webster and Tourneur.** Introduction by JOHN ADDINGTON SYMONDS.

13 and 14. **The Best Plays of Thomas Middleton.** Introduction by ALGERNON CHARLES SWINBURNE.

15. **The Best Plays of James Shirley.** Introduction by EDMUND GOSSE.

16. **The Best Plays of Thomas Dekker.** Notes by ERNEST RHYS.

17, 19, and 20. **The Best Plays of Ben Jonson.** Vol. I. edited, with Introduction and Notes, by BRINSLEY NICHOLSON and C. H. HERFORD.

18. **The Complete Plays of Richard Steele.** Edited, with Introduction and Notes, by G. A. AITKEN.

21. **The Best Plays of George Chapman.** Edited by WILLIAM LYON PHELPS, Instructor of English Literature at Yale College.

22. **The Select Plays of Sir John Vanbrugh.** Edited, with an Introduction and Notes, by A. E. H. SWAEN.

PRESS OPINIONS.

"Even the professed scholar with a good library at his command will find some texts here not otherwise easily accessible; while the humbler student of slender resources, who knows the bitterness of not being able to possess himself of the treasure stored in expensive folios or quartos long out of print, will assuredly rise up and thank Mr. Unwin."—*St. James's Gazette.*

"Resumed under good auspices."—*Saturday Review.*

"The issue is as good as it could be."—*British Weekly.*

"At once scholarly and interesting."—*Leeds Mercury.*

T. FISHER UNWIN, Publisher,

THE STORY OF
THE NATIONS

A SERIES OF POPULAR HISTORIES.

Each Volume is furnished with Maps, Illustrations, and Index. Large Crown 8vo., fancy cloth, gold lettered, or Library Edition, dark cloth, burnished red top, **5s.** *each.—Or may be had in half Persian, cloth sides, gilt tops; Price on Application.*

1. **Rome.** By ARTHUR GILMAN, M.A.
2. **The Jews.** By Professor J. K. HOSMER.
3. **Germany.** By the Rev. S. BARING-GOULD.
4. **Carthage.** By Professor ALFRED J. CHURCH.
5. **Alexander's Empire.** By Prof. J. P. MAHAFFY.
6. **The Moors in Spain.** By STANLEY LANE-POOLE.
7. **Ancient Egypt.** By Prof. GEORGE RAWLINSON.
8. **Hungary.** By Prof. ARMINIUS VAMBERY.
9. **The Saracens.** By ARTHUR GILMAN, M.A.
10. **Ireland.** By the Hon. EMILY LAWLESS.
11. **Chaldea.** By ZENAIDE A. RAGOZIN.
12. **The Goths.** By HENRY BRADLEY.
13. **Assyria.** By ZENAIDE A. RAGOZIN.
14. **Turkey.** By STANLEY LANE-POOLE.
15. **Holland.** By Professor J. E. THOROLD ROGERS.
16. **Mediæval France.** By GUSTAVE MASSON.
17. **Persia.** By S. G. W. BENJAMIN.
18. **Phœnicia.** By Prof. GEORGE RAWLINSON.
19. **Media.** By ZENAIDE A. RAGOZIN.
20. **The Hansa Towns.** By HELEN ZIMMERN.
21. **Early Britain.** By Professor ALFRED J. CHURCH.
22. **The Barbary Corsairs.** By STANLEY LANE-POOLE.
23. **Russia.** By W. R. MORFILL.
24. **The Jews under the Roman Empire.** By W. D. MORRISON.
25. **Scotland.** By JOHN MACKINTOSH, LL.D.
26. **Switzerland.** By R. STEAD and LINA HUG.
27. **Mexico.** By SUSAN HALE.
28. **Portugal.** By H. MORSE STEPHENS.
29. **The Normans.** By SARAH ORNE JEWETT.
30. **The Byzantine Empire.** By C. W. C. OMAN, M.A.
31. **Sicily: Phœnician, Greek and Roman.** By the late E. A. FREEMAN.
32. **The Tuscan and Genoa Republics.** By BELLA DUFFY.
33. **Poland.** By W. R. MORFILL.
34. **Parthia.** By Prof. GEORGE RAWLINSON.
35. **The Australian Commonwealth.** By GREVILLE TREGARTHEN.
36. **Spain.** By H. E. WATTS.
37. **Japan.** By DAVID MURRAY, Ph.D.
38. **South Africa.** By GEORGE M. THEAL.
39. **Venice.** By the Hon. ALETHEA WIEL.
40. **The Crusades:** The Latin Kingdom of Jerusalem. By T. A. ARCHER and CHARLES L. KINGSFORD.
41. **Vedic India.** By ZENAIDE A. RAGOZIN.
42. **The West Indies and the Spanish Main.** By JAMES RODWAY, F.L.S.
43. **Bohemia.** By C. E. MAURICE.
44. **The Balkans.** By W. MILLER.
45. **Canada.** By Dr. BOURINOT.
46. **British India.** By R. W. FRAZER, LL.B.
47. **Modern France.** By ANDRÉ LE BON.
   The Franks. By LEWIS SERGEANT, B.A.

"Such a universal history as the series will present us with in its completion will be a possession such as no country but our own can boast of. . . . Its success on the whole has been very remarkable."—*Daily Chronicle.*

11, Paternoster Buildings, London, E.C.

T. FISHER UNWIN, Publisher,

THE CHILDREN'S STUDY

• • •

Long 8vo., cloth, gilt top, with photogravure frontispiece, price **2/6** *each.*

1. **Scotland.** By Mrs. OLIPHANT.
2. **Ireland.** Edited by BARRY O'BRIEN.
3. **England.** By FRANCES E. COOKE.
4. **Germany.** By KATE FREILIGRATH KROEKER, Author of "Fairy Tales from Brentano," &c.
5. **Old Tales from Greece.** By ALICE ZIMMERN.
6. **France.** By MARY ROWSELL.
7. **The United States.** By MINNA SMITH.
8. **Rome.** By MARY FORD.

OPINIONS OF THE PRESS ON "SCOTLAND."

"For children of the right age this is an excellent little history."—*Daily News.*

"Enough of fault-finding with a writer who has otherwise performed his task in a perfectly charming manner."—*Daily Chronicle.*

"The best book for the rising Caledonian that has appeared for many a day."

"Simple, picturesque, and well-proportioned."—*Glasgow Herald.*   [*Scotsman.*

"A charming book full of life and colour."—*Speaker.*

"As a stimulator of the imagination and intelligence, it is a long way ahead of many books in use in some schools."—*Sketch.*

"The book is attractively produced. Mrs. Oliphant has performed her difficult task well."—*Educational Times.*

"A work which may claim its place upon the shelves of the young people's library, where it may prove of not a little service also to their elders."—*School Board Chronicle.*

OPINIONS OF THE PRESS ON "IRELAND."

"Many who are children no longer will be glad of this compact but able introduction to the story of Ireland's woes. The form of the volume is particularly attractive."
British Weekly.

"We heartily congratulate Mr. Barry O'Brien upon this interesting little volume. The style is intensely interesting."—*Schoolmaster.*

"It is well that the youth of England, who have entered into a serious inheritance and who will soon be the voters of England, should have some conception of the country with whom they are so closely bound up, and for whose past their fathers are so heavily responsible. We do not know of any work so fitting for imparting to them this knowledge as the present, which, therefore, we heartily commend to all teachers as the best text-book of Irish history for the young."—*Daily Chronicle.*

OPINIONS OF THE PRESS ON "ENGLAND."

"Terse, vivid, well-informed."—*Speaker.*

"Pleasantly written, and well within the capacity of a young child. . . . We anticipate with pleasure the appearance of the succeeding volumes of 'The Children's Study.'"—*School Guardian.*

"Admirably done . . . . always easy of understanding."—*Scotsman.*

OPINIONS OF THE PRESS ON "GERMANY."

"We have seldom seen a small history so well balanced, and consequently so adequate as an introduction to the subject."—*Educational Times.*

"Painstaking and well written."—*Daily Chronicle.*

"Clear as accurate. It is just the sort of book to give to a youngster who has to study Teutonic history."—*Black and White.*

"An interesting historical series."—*Pall Mall Gazette.*

11, Paternoster Buildings, London, E.C.   *aa*

T. FISHER UNWIN, Publisher,

BUILDERS OF GREATER BRITAIN

EDITED BY

H. F. WILSON

A Set of 10 Volumes, each with Photogravure Frontispiece, and Map, large crown 8vo., cloth, 5s. each.

The completion of the Sixtieth year of the Queen's reign will be the occasion of much retrospect and review, in the course of which the great men who, under the auspices of Her Majesty and her predecessors, have helped to make the British Empire what it is to-day, will naturally be brought to mind. Hence the idea of the present series. These biographies, concise but full, popular but authoritative, have been designed with the view of giving in each case an adequate picture of the builder in relation to his work.

The series will be under the general editorship of Mr. H. F. Wilson, formerly Fellow of Trinity College, Cambridge, and now private secretary to the Right Hon. J. Chamberlain at the Colonial Office. Each volume will be placed in competent hands, and will contain the best portrait obtainable of its subject, and a map showing his special contribution to the Imperial edifice. The first to appear will be a Life of Sir Walter Ralegh, by Major Hume, the learned author of "The Year after the Armada." Others in contemplation will deal with the Cabots, the quarter-centenary of whose sailing from Bristol is has recently been celebrated in that city, as well as in Canada and Newfoundland ; Sir Thomas Maitland, the "King Tom" of the Mediterranean ; Rajah Brooke, Sir Stamford Raffles, Lord Clive, Edward Gibbon Wakefield, Zachary Macaulay, &c., &c.

The Series has taken for its motto the Miltonic prayer :—

" Thou Who of Thy free grace didst build up this Brittannick Empire to a glorious and enviable height, with all her Daughter Islands about her, stay us in this felicitie."

1. **SIR WALTER RALEGH.** By MARTIN A. S. HUME, Author of "The Courtships of Queen Elizabeth," &c.

2. **SIR THOMAS MAITLAND;** the Mastery of the Mediterranean. By WALTER FREWEN LORD.

3. **JOHN CABOT AND HIS SONS;** the Discovery of North America. By C. RAYMOND BEAZLEY, M.A.

4. **LORD CLIVE;** the Foundation of British Rule in India. By Sir A. J. ARBUTHNOT, K.C.S.I., C.I.E.

5. **EDWARD GIBBON WAKEFIELD;** the Colonisation of South Australia and New Zealand. By R. GARNETT, C.B., LL.D.

6. **RAJAH BROOKE;** the Englishman as Ruler of an Eastern State. By Sir SPENSER ST. JOHN, G.C.M.G

7. **ADMIRAL PHILIP;** the Founding of New South Wales. By LOUIS BECKE and WALTER JEFFERY.

8. **SIR STAMFORD RAFFLES;** England in the Far East. By the Editor.

T. FISHER UNWIN, Publisher,

MASTERS OF MEDICINE

EDITED BY

ERNEST HART, D.C.L.,

Editor of "The British Medical Journal."

Large crown 8vo., cloth, **3s. 6d.** *each.*

Medical discoveries more directly concern the well-being and happiness of the human race than any victories of science. They appeal to one of the primary instincts of human nature, that of self-preservation. The importance of health as the most valuable of our national assets is coming to be more and more recognised, and the place of the doctor in Society and in the State is becoming one of steadily increasing prominence; indeed, Mr. Gladstone said not many years ago that the time would surely come when the medical profession would take precedence of all the others in authority as well as in dignity. The development of medicine from an empiric art to an exact science is one of the most important and also one of the most interesting chapters in the history of civilisation. The histories of medicine which exist are for the most part only fitted for the intellectual digestion of Dryasdust and his congeners. Of the men who made the discoveries which have saved incalculable numbers of human lives, and which have lengthened the span of human existence, there is often no record at all accessible to the general reader. Yet the story of these men's lives, of their struggles and of their triumphs, is not only interesting, but in the highest degree stimulating and educative. Many of them could have said with literal truth what Sir Thomas Browne said figuratively, that their lives were a romance. Hitherto there have been no accounts of the lives of medical discoverers in a form at once convenient and uniform, and sold at a popular price. The "Masters of Medicine" is a series of biographies written by "eminent hands" intended to supply this want. It is intended that the man shall be depicted as he moved and lived and had his being, and that the scope and gist of his work, as well as the steps by which he reached his results, shall be set forth in a clear, readable style.

The following is a condensed list of some of the earlier volumes :—

11, Paternoster Buildings, London, E.C. *dd*